Mount II

The Next Adventure

Arlen Blumhagen

Untreed
Reads

Mount II: The Next Adventure
By Arlen Blumhagen

Copyright 2017 by Arlen Blumhagen
Cover Copyright 2017 by Untreed Reads Publishing
Cover Design by Ginny Glass

ISBN-13: 978-1-94544-756-3

Also available in ebook format.

Published by Untreed Reads, LLC
506 Kansas Street, San Francisco, CA 94107

www.untreedreads.com

Printed in the United States of America.

Publisher's Note

This is a work of fiction. Names, characters, places, and incidents either are the product of the author's imagination or are used fictitiously, and any resemblance to actual persons, living or dead, business establishments, events, or locales is entirely coincidental.

The publisher does not have any control over and does not assume any responsibility for author or third-party websites or their content.

Chapter One

Howdy. Folks call me Mount. Those that don't don't know me. My folks pinned Thaddeus Beauregard Battner on me at birth. Now, Pa bein' named Christopher and Ma bein' Sara, God only knows why they'd do such a thing to their own, but over the years ain't nobody paid much attention anyway.

I'm just Mount. Mostly 'cause I ended up mountain sized at around six and a half feet tall, and when I look down at two hundred pounds, it's half a day's ride. I'm big, hairy, and ugly as a damned warthog. Close as I can figure, I reckon I'm somewhere in my mid-thirties.

Now, how the hell those two city folks that raised me up, made it from St. Louis, Missouri clear across the country to that beautiful meadow at the foot of those majestic mountains without gettin' themselves killed is a downright miracle.

Pa had read some accounts of them fellers, Lewis and Clark, who'd been explorin' out west. Pa got his self all worked up thinkin' about the adventure and excitement, things sorely lacking in his life as a store owner's son. He just had to go see for himself.

When they left St. Louis bound for that new and exciting life out west, Pa knew about as much on the subject of livin' off the land and surviving in the wilderness as I do about this New York City that I keep hearin' tell of.

The good Lord musta been ridin' with them a big stretch of the way 'cause make it they did; and I'm powerful thankful for it.

I was raised up in the small log cabin that my folks built when they settled in this valley back around 1815. The cabin sits in the shadows of a small range of the great Rocky Mountains. Beside the cabin runs Sweetgrass Creek (Pa named it) which empties into the mighty Yellowstone River a mile or so downstream.

The grass, sweet clover, and wildflower filled meadow above the cabin stretches out and runs up against mostly pine covered foothills. Those rolling hills grow and reach for the sky until they climb up above the tree line. From there naked granite soars up into jagged mountain peaks. Up there where the snow stays put all year-round.

I'm mighty proud and happy to still be livin' in Pa's cabin, although I did hear tell of some folks settlin' down not fifty miles due east of my meadow. Now, if folks start to crowdin' me like that, I might be forced to meander up north.

I learned most of what I needed to know by followin' Pa around the high-country and backwoods as he hunted, fished, and trapped to provide for his family.

My book learnin' came from Ma. She'd been a schoolteacher back in St. Louis, and insisted that I learn proper readin' and writin'.

My schooling in the fundamental things in life; things like fighting, gambling, whiskey drinkin', and those unmentionables that I ain't gonna mention, I learned at Rendezvous. Twice a year, in spring and fall, for most of my life I've made that four day ride south to Fort Granger for some socializin' and serious hell raisin' at Rendezvous.

*

One bitter cold morning back in the winter of 1838 Pa left to check his trap lines and didn't come home. Ma could never accept the fact that he was gone. It didn't take but a year or so before she joined him in the great beyond. As much as she loved me and our life in that beautiful valley, she loved Pa more and needed to be with him.

Ma's dyin' led to the first real journey (other than Rendezvous) of my life. Figurin' it was the right thing to do, I tied my bedroll onto my pony, Skyhawk, and we made our way clear to St. Louis to inform their families of Ma and Pa's passing. Surprisingly we made the trip without gettin' lost or killed.

There wasn't much family left in St. Louis, only Pa's mother and brother. Grandma Battner was so old and feeble that I wasn't sure if she even knew I was there, but when I told her that her son had passed on, a single tear rolled down her cheek. By the time it made its way through all the valleys and crevasses to her chin she was back asleep and snorin' softly.

In addition to meeting my uncle Joseph Battner, who still ran the family's business, I was unfortunate enough to make the acquaintance of a gentleman by the name of Mr. Andrew Worthington the Second.

Mr. Worthington was an extremely rich, incredibly arrogant bastard of a businessman who, against my better judgment, convinced me to guide him and his family back across the country to Oregon City.

Some of you may've read the story.

It was a damned miracle; actually it took several miracles, before I eventually got those folks where they intended to go.

My heart still aches some when I allow myself to think about certain participants of that great cross-country adventure.

It'd been nearly two years after I got back to my mountain cabin when I found myself caught up in a new, even more dangerous venture; one that would have its own heartaches and see its own miracles.

Chapter Two

Early last fall, that'd be the fall of 1843, I made my way down to Fort Granger for Rendezvous. I had one of the finest harvests of furs and pelts that I've ever harvested, and I was ready for one of the best damn times ever at Rendezvous, and that's sayin' something.

You probably think that if I could've foreseen the sorrow and difficulties that lay in store, I would've stayed away, safe and warm in my mountain cabin.

I reckon most folks spend some time wanderin' through Hell before they find their way to Heaven. Taking into account how it all turned out, I guess given the choice I'd do it all again. And I say that with apologies to my good friend Patch Willis.

I'd sure as hell change some parts if I was given the chance.

*

The excitement started when I was still a full day shy of Fort Granger.

It was early fall and the trees had just started to show off their autumn finery. The foothills I rode through were mostly covered with evergreens; ponderosa pine down low changing over to lodgepole pine up higher, but every now and then there'd be a stand of aspen or maple with the box elder, cottonwoods, and willows following the creeks and riverbeds.

All those leafy trees were wearin' their fall ceremonial dress, and they surely prettied up the day as the sun seemed to light 'em on fire. The whole danged countryside was showin' off leaves of brilliant colors ranging from sunflower yellow, through gold and orange, to dark blood red. They all shined brightly amidst all the different shades of green; and fluttered in a gentle wind.

The mountains towered to snow covered peaks to my right. I rode through the forested hills and past miles of sandstone cliffs

5

that soared a hundred feet or more into the big blue sky and had been cut and carved into the most peculiar shapes by thousands of years of brutal weather.

Goldfire, the magnificent Palomino stallion that I'd received as payment from Mr. Worthington, and I was moseyin' along just enjoying the cool weather and beautiful scenery. My packhorse, loaded down with hides and pelts, was on a loose guide rope and followed behind.

I was plenty warm and content wearin' heavy new deerskins. My rabbit-fur hat was pulled down tight. The light breeze tugged at my beard and the hair that stuck out under my hat, and was filled with the refreshing smell of pine and mountains.

Suddenly, from the dense pine forest to my right, comes a scream like there was a wild banshee on the loose. Goldfire drew up all on his own and we prepared for the worst.

What we got was a young Indian girl, ridin' hell-bent outta the trees and headed straight for me. My packhorse spooked and I had to tighten the lead rope to bring her under control.

As the young lady skidded to a stop beside us another horse broke from the trees in pursuit.

"Help me mister!" The young Indian girl cried. "Please help me! Don't let that bastard get me!" I noticed there wasn't so much as a hint of Indian accent.

The horse bearin' down on us was a big bay mare. On her back were a buffalo robe and a coonskin hat with the sides pulled down and tied. I could only assume that there was a person in there somewhere; and judging from the girl's actions, a dangerous person.

That Indian gal nudged her pony and scrambled around behind us so we were between her and her pursuer. I turned to face whatever challenge was comin' at me.

"Get the hell out'a my way boy!" The voice was deep and rumbling, like a rockslide. "I'll ride ya down!"

As big as that mare was, Goldfire was at least two hands taller. He and I braced for the collision.

At the last instant Buffalo Robe jerked sideways on the reins and tried to guide his horse around us.

I didn't even think before I reacted. A problem I've been plagued with most of my born days.

As that big horse raced past I jerked my left foot outta the stirrup, shifted my weight over onto my right leg, and dove. I wrapped my arms around that buffalo robe and rode it to the ground like I was bulldoggin' in the rodeo.

When we hit the ground the wind exploded out of Buffalo Robe like it'd been dynamited. The coonskin hat buried itself down into the robe's chest, and robe covered arms wrapped around it for protection.

I figured to take full advantage of the fact that my adversary was momentarily out of wind. Before we'd even stopped bouncin' I was up on one knee trying to pummel the bastard with my fists. All I hit was buffalo hide.

"Mou..." A muffled cry told me that he'd gotten his breath back. I increased the intensity of my attack.

"Mount." Was that what it'd sounded like? "Mount, quit hilttl..." Just knowin' my name didn't mean spit.

I got one more good punch in at the back of that damned coonskin hat before pain erupted at the base of my neck and raced up and down my spine like a wildfire in a strong wind. Suddenly I was slumped over my foe, unable to move a damn muscle; a hot, tingly feeling traveled like waves on a pond, up and down my body.

"Leave my pa alone!"

I couldn't move, but I sure as hell could feel the beatin' that young lady continued to inflict about my back and shoulders. The balled up buffalo hide underneath me was getting his voice back.

"Mount...it's Patch!" He still wasn't taking any chances by uncovering his head. "Patch...Patch Willis."

Of course, I'd stopped hitting him when my arms quit workin', but Patch didn't know due to the fact that that damn Indian girl kept beating on me which kept jostlin' him.

"Call off your squaw."

"Sunshine." I even recognized his voice now. "Sunny, leave the man alone now."

"Nobody hurts Pa!" The young woman exclaimed as she got in one more good, solid whack across my shoulders. I saw she was using a three foot tree limb. She dropped it and stepped back.

The ability to move my arms and legs slowly started coming back, accompanied by what felt like a million bee stings all up and down my body. I rolled off Patch and moved away from the girl like a baby just learnin' to crawl. I didn't know if I could trust my legs, so I didn't try; I stayed on the ground.

"Wheee haw!" Patch Willis sat up and pulled the coonskin from his head. Shoulder length gray hair tumbled out covering most of his face. "Damn, Mount, we was just funnin' with ya. You didn't need to get so damned rough." Patch pulled his hair back with both hands as he turned to the Indian girl. "And I ain't your pa, so stop sayin' so. Hell, I ain't near old enough to be your pa."

"Buffalo chips, Patch!" I was workin' the feeling back into my arms. "Hell, you're old enough to be *my* pa. I'd say you got some explainin' to do." As I made my speech, I slowly climbed to my feet and stood with one hand holding on to Goldfire for support; with the other I rubbed the knot on the back of my head where the girl had hit me and numbed me up. There wasn't much blood, but it hurt like hell. "Damn it, Patch. What in tarnation are you up to?"

Patch Willis, of course, was a mountain man. He'd been stoppin' by the cabin every couple of years for as long back as I could remember. And he was nearly always at Rendezvous. He wasn't a big man, I doubt he reached to six feet, but he was hard as granite. I counted Patch among my small number of friends.

"Well shoot, Mount." I offered my hand to help him to his feet. He came up bowed over and needed both hands to support his back as he straightened. "We was over yonder restin' the horses and preparin' some grub when I saw you ride into the clearing. It was obvious that you weren't payin' no attention at all. I thought your pa taught you better than that, Mount." He was right, Pa *had* taught me better. "I had Sunny ride out actin' like she needed help, thinkin' to get ya worked up a little." Patch was finally standing straight, his right hand rubbing at that sore spot on his lower back. "Hell, I didn't figure you was gonna rip me off my horse like you did."

"Yeah, I didn't know either, till I done it."

I took my first good look at that little Indian gal. She was squatted back on her haunches and starin' at me real mean like. Looking like she wouldn't mind smackin' me up side the head another time or two. She was a pretty girl, probably a little older than I first thought. My guess was that she was only half Indian, half somethin' else.

"What the hell you lookin' at?"

"Well, I was just..."

"Sunny, you behave now." Patch was checking the rigging on his saddle, makin' sure nothing had come loose. "Mount is a friend."

"He was hurtin' you."

"Yeah, well." Patch rubbed his sore back again. "That was mostly a miscalculation on my part."

He stepped over and slapped me on the back. "I've known Mount Battner since his ma wrapped his butt in flour sacks. Mount's pa, Christopher, and I trapped and hunted together many a time." Satisfied that his saddle wasn't going to slide off as he got on, Patch mounted his bay mare. "Follow us yonder, Mount." He pointed across the small clearing. "We'll have some grub and lie to each other for a spell. You headed to Rendezvous?"

"Yep." My nerves had finally settled. I was happy for the company. "You headed that way?" I got on Goldfire.

"Yep."

*

Not long after, we was gathered around a small campfire. There were a couple of large rabbits on a spit, cookin' real slow above the hot coals.

Sunny was coming back from doing her business and as she cleared some juniper bushes I pointed to a large, dead pine limb layin' on the ground beside her.

"Grab that firewood." I didn't mean a damn thing by it. The wood was there and she was there; just made sense to me.

She sneered down at the log, then held the sneer as she looked at me.

"I ain't your damn slave!"

"I didn't mean...I just..."

"You too lazy to get your own wood, old man?"

Now that little Indian girl was gettin' me riled up. "Old man? Why, I should... Nobody ever paddled any respect into you when you was young did they?"

She was to the fire ring by then. That little slip of a thing squared off in front of me with her feet apart and her hands on her hips. I thought maybe I could actually see lightning flash in her eyes.

"You plannin' to try?"

"Hell no!" I couldn't help but snicker a little. Patch was shakin' his head and rollin' his eyes. "I ain't never been one to lay hand on a female." I looked the girl up and down. On her toes she maybe stretched a sliver over five feet, and weighted about the same as a newborn fawn. "And I sure as hell ain't gonna start with a female that's liable to whoop my ass."

Sunny seemed to like my answer. I think I even saw a trace of a smile as she turned and went to pick up the limb. She got it and then made a circle collecting more.

"How the hell did you end up with that polecat?" I asked Patch.

He'd taken his buffalo robe off and I was reminded of where Patch had gotten his nickname.

When he was still a young man he'd learned the art of sewing from an old Indian woman. Since then I don't think he'd ever made a new set of clothes. He just patched the old ones as they wore out. His deer hide shirt had a buffalo hide piece across the back, a beaver pelt shoulder, and what I guessed was coyote made up the left sleeve. The pants had different legs, and I'm pretty sure the butt was rabbit fur.

"I was up north." Patch settled himself beside the fire. "Way up north. There's a tradin' post up there where the Clearwater and Athabasca Rivers join up."

Sunny carried over a large armful of wood, threw it beside the fire and sat down.

"The proprietor of the General store there, and his wife, had been providing for her..."

"Takin' advantage of her, you mean." Sunny punched the air. "That ole bitty made me work my ass off."

"Samuel, the proprietor, said she'd been there for at least fifteen years and was walkin' and talkin' when they took her in."

As Patch talked I dug into my bedroll and pulled out a small canteen. Patch's nose twitched and his eyes lit up when he got a whiff.

I took a long healthy swig of the whiskey and as it burned its way down I handed the canteen to Patch. He enjoyed a swallow before continuing. Sunny watched us expectantly, but we ignored her.

"They figured her ma was a local Cree Indian. Some folks claim to've known her pa. They say he was a Frenchman prospectin' for gold. I figure he was the one that raised her until he decided it was time to move on. He probably figured she'd be better off with white folks. Indians tend to be awful hard on half-breeds. Nobody knew her name. Samuel's wife, Lilly, took to callin' her Sunshine."

"And that all explains her, but it don't explain why she's ridin' with you."

Patch and Sunny exchanged a look; a look that said they had a secret. He just shook his head and shrugged his shoulders like there wasn't any explainin' to do.

"Because I wanted to." Sunny spoke up. Patch nodded his head and smiled.

"That's about it." He looked at me and shrugged again. "When she found out I was headin' down to Rendezvous, she begged to come along and..."

"I ain't never begged for nothin'! I just asked...a few times."

"Samuel and Lilly had been havin' a time of it keeping the young bucks from sniffin' and pawin' around her so they thought it might be best for her to move on."

"Shoot, I gotta be near twenty years old." Some of the fight had left her eyes and had been replaced by excitement. "I ain't never been anywhere before." Anger suddenly flashed in her eyes. "And besides, that ole hag never did like me. If it wouldn't have been for Samuel she would've kicked me out long ago."

"That 'ole hag' bawled like a baby when you left."

"Ahh, hell." Suddenly Sunny looked like she was close to tears herself. "Those were tears of joy. She was just happy to see me go is all." Sunny stared into the fire, unwilling to look at either of us.

"And now that you got her," I'd turned back to Patch. "What do you do with her?"

"I'll do for myself, thank you very much!"

"I didn't mean nothin' by it, I just..."

"I been takin' care of myself since forever."

"I just..."

"I'm gonna ride with Patch to Rendezvous and then I'm gonna find some real rich folks that need a girl to do things for them. And I'm gonna spend the rest of my life livin' with rich folks and doin' for them."

"Well now," I grinned, and stared into the fire. "I know a thing or two about workin' for rich folks, and let me tell you it ain't all lavender water and big juicy steaks." I remembered a couple of the ranting fits that Mr. Worthington the Second had had during our cross-country adventure. "They can be a real challenge at times."

Memories of Mr. Worthington's wife, Sandra, and their teenage son, Andy, flooded my thoughts, washing away the ugly images of a furious Mr. Worthington and replacing them with joyful memories; joyful memories that hurt just a little bit.

"Although, some rich folks," I recalled watching a naked Sandra wade into the river for a bath, "can be mighty fine people."

I remembered Andy sittin' in the dirt laughing so hard he couldn't talk after being thrown from Skyhawk. "Some can even become damn good friends."

"Well, that's what I'm gonna do anyway." Sunny spoke as if the deed was already done. "I'm gonna live with some rich folks that'll treat me just like one of their own."

By the time Patch and I had gotten all caught up, and all our lies told, it was time to make camp for the night, so we decided to stay.

After a few more stories and a couple more snorts of whiskey (we even let Sunny have a swallow), we stretched out beside the fire, wrapped up in our blankets, and slept.

The three of us rode into Fort Granger and Rendezvous the next day.

Chapter Three

The first three days at Rendezvous were fine and dandy; just like they're suppose to be.

By the end of the second day I'd traded off most of my goods; and wrangled a fair price for most everything too. It seemed the demand for skins, furs, and pelts was booming back east, and across the ocean in some place they called the United Kingdom.

After my tradin' was done and my supplies stored away I got down to business. The serious business of eatin', drinkin', and womanizin' way more than is healthy for a feller.

There ain't a mountain man alive or dead that'd even consider a different way of life, but every one of 'em will admit that it can get a might lonely now and again. Spendin' a few days amongst people a couple times a year is a right nice change of pace.

Any more than five days and most mountain folks can't wait to be alone again.

I believe it was the morning of the fourth day, but I wouldn't bet a gold nugget on it. I was comin' out of the Trail's End Saloon. They had rooms to rent upstairs. The price included two drinks, a tub of hot water, and a whore.

I was movin' kinda slow 'cause my head was packed with mud and my gut with squirming snakes.

I planned on using Goldfire to win some races and horsemanship competitions later in the day, but first I was in desperate need of grub and hot coffee.

"Mount!" My head snapped up fast at the panic in her voice. Pain shot down my spine. "Mount, help!"

I turned to see Sunny runnin' from the boarding house across the way. Close behind her, but losing ground now that she was out in the open, were three real mean lookin' hombres.

"Mount, help! They hurt Patch! Hurt him real bad!"

As soon as she saw me head her way Sunny stopped runnin'. She turned and squared up to those three renegades and prepared to take 'em on.

Now, I ain't sure if it was my six and a half feet lumberin' towards them, or if it was that five foot cyclone that faced 'em down, but those fellers decided against whatever they'd had planned. All three turned tail and scurried back into the boardinghouse.

"Come on, Mount!" Sunny was already sprinting for the door that the men had just gone through. "We have to help Patch. They hurt him Mount, hurry!"

I knew I could fight if pressed to, but run? My body was so tuckered out from three days of abusing it that walkin' was a chore. Runnin' across the street and into that boarding house was pure torture.

The three men that had been chasin' Sunny stood on the other side of the room, near a door. Two were white and one was Mexican.

In the center of the room lay Patch. He was on his side with his knees drawn up and his arms circled around his head. There was blood on the floor and on his hands.

Down on one knee beside him was another Mexican. That feller wore a colorful vest, a red bandana around his neck, and a wide-brimmed sombrero. He'd been looking back at the other three men when Sunny hit the front door like a runaway bull.

When he saw her the feller beside Patch took to hollerin' and pointin'. He bolted upright and took a couple steps forward, gesturing to his friends to follow.

When I trailed Sunny through the door, Mr. Fancy Vest had second thoughts too. He glanced back over his shoulder and saw that the three men had abandoned him through the door.

He turned and hurried to follow his friends. Sunny let out an inhumane screech, took about three running steps, and leapt onto the fleeing Mexican's back. She hung on with one hand and began to pummel his head and scratch at his face with the other.

He planted his right foot and twisted violently to the left. Sunny slid and ended up with her head pokin' over his shoulder. A vicious elbow sent her flying to land at my feet just as I reached out to grab a hold of the bastard. By the time I made sure Sunny was okay, and had stepped over her to give chase, the coward was gone.

That tough little half-breed gal was already climbing to her feet when I turned around. One hand pinched her nose. Blood trickled between her fingers.

Movement and a loud groan brought my attention back to Patch. He had rolled onto his back. Both hands still covered his face.

Sunny and I got to him about the same time. Patch jerked away in fear when Sunny laid her hand on his arm.

"It's okay, Patch." She squeezed his arm reassuringly. "They're gone, Patch. It's okay."

He took his hands away from his face and slowly opened his eyes. Well, one opened. The other was already swelled shut. There was a bad cut above the swelled eye, and his lower lip had been split open. My two eyes met his one.

"Thanks, Mount."

"Hell, I didn't do anything." I laughed. "They ran like the Devil himself was after 'em when they saw how mad Sunny was."

Patch's eyes drifted over to Sunny, and his split lips pulled back into a painful smile. Sunny sat on the floor pinching her bleeding nose and grinning.

*

A half hour later we had Patch back in his room, and most of the blood cleaned up. Sunny's nose had quit bleedin' and she was working on patchin' up Patch. Besides the split lip and battered eye, he also had a nasty gash on the top of his head where he had a very limited amount of hair for protection. It was the head wound that had caused most of the blood. And there may've been a cracked rib or two; Patch said it hurt like hell to take a deep breath.

"That Chavez is a bad one." Patch shook his head.

"Sit still." Sunny was cleaning on the cut above his eye.

Turned out that the Mexican with the fancy clothes was Juan Chavez, and this hadn't been the first time Patch and Sunny had had to deal with him and his cronies.

"Sunny may've forgotten a couple small details about what happened up north." Patch said. Sunny paused in her doctorin'. "Why she's ridin' with me."

"I forgot?!" Sunny exclaimed. "But, Patch, you said not to…"

"I reckon the time's come to tell you the whole of it, huh?" Patch interrupted her.

"I'm here to listen, Patch." I still planned to run Goldfire in a couple races, but I had some time. All the excitement had taken care of my hangover.

"Chavez is plumb loco over Sunny." The glance Patch gave Sunny held all the love of a father for his daughter. "From the second he laid eyes on her up north he was smitten. He had to have her. And Juan Chavez is used to gettin' what he wants."

"I'll die first!" Sunny had that ole familiar lightning flashing in her eyes. She'd finished doctorin' Patch and was sitting beside us.

"After Sunny had rejected him twice in public, once in the store and another time in the saloon, Chavez changed his tactics." Patch didn't tend to show his emotions much, but he was having a hard time controlling them. "He decided to kidnap her."

"They came right into my room. They caught me off guard." Sunny took over the story. "Grabbed me and hauled me down the stairs and right out the front door."

"I just happened to be ridin' past when the door flew open and them sidewinders came carryin' Sunny out. She was screamin' and kickin' and raisin' one hell of a ruckus. Several, supposedly good, upstanding citizens, just stood there and watched." Patch continued. "Chavez was already mounted, waiting for his henchmen to do his dirty work. I drew my flintlock, and got the drop on 'em."

"When he saw that long-gun pointed at him," Sunny's eyes were again filled with excitement. "All the courage drained out of him like a leaky bucket. One word from Patch and they let me go in a hurry."

"Hell, that damned rifle weren't even primed to fire." Patch chuckled, and then his eyes got real narrow and serious like. "I knew there'd be more trouble from that bunch. I was fixin' to leave anyway, so I talked to Samuel and Lilly about gettin' Sunny out of there, so…"

"I would've come anyway!" Sunny put on her determined face. "Whether you said I could or not. I would've followed you if I needed to."

Patch looked me square in the eyes.

"After what happened today," he said, "ain't no doubt there's gonna be more trouble. I guarantee it. And now you're part of it, Mount." The sincerity and concern in his voice warmed my heart. "You best stay clear of the two of us." He looked at Sunny. "Better yet, I think the two of us might just head out. Mosey back up north. Maybe go west through the mountains and meander over Oregon City way."

My heart raced at just the mention of Oregon City. I couldn't help but think of the friends (and enemies) I'd left there.

"Tell you what." I'd done everything that needed gettin' done at Rendezvous, and I'd already abused my body more than a feller ought to. "I got no reason to travel to Oregon City, but I'll ride north with you for a couple days until you head west over Mullin Pass. If Chavez and his men are plannin' something, they'll make their move by then."

"Mount, there's no need for you to…"

"I've had enough Rendezvous." And I mostly meant it. "I don't think Chavez has the guts to confront the three of us." I was sorta right. "There's this loudmouth here at the fort braggin' up his horse, a big black stallion. Goldfire and I aim to show him a thing or two. After that I'm ready to hit the trail."

"Okay, Mount." Patch smiled sincerely. "I'm mighty beholdin' to ya. Thanks." He turned to Sunny. "Let's get packed up and ready to ride."

Sunny's quest to find some rich folks at Rendezvous had worked out just fine. There were two families who qualified.

Her plan to get hired on and spend the rest of her life livin' in luxury with them didn't pan out quite as well. Although both husbands were willing to consider the possibility, neither family ended up showing much interest at all in having a beautiful half-breed girl to do for them.

The horserace went exactly the way I figured it would. It was a short race, just a quarter mile. The start was a quarter mile out on a wagon trail. The finish line was even with the first building of the Fort Granger settlement. And there were people lining both sides of the track the whole way.

Mr. Loudmouth with the black stallion ate Goldfire's dust the whole way. We beat him by nearly three lengths. There were other longer races later in the day, and Goldfire and I would've won those too, but we didn't stay.

After the race I met Patch and Sunny at the livery stable. It took me ten minutes to load my packhorse, and we were on our way. I watched close for any sign of Chavez or his friends. I didn't see anything.

Chapter Four

The yellowbellied cowards hit us the second night out. We were most of the way across the plains, camped in a small stand of aspen above a fast moving creek that had cut a nearly twenty foot deep course through the dirt and sandstone.

The next day we would've reached the southern arm of the mountains; one of many smaller chains that all together make up the great Rocky Mountains.

That's where Patch and Sunny would've turned west, over the mountains towards Oregon City, and I'd continue north, back home to my cabin. Only we didn't make it there.

I'd stood first watch. Now, I don't know where those bastards were hidin', but not only me, but Goldfire (whose senses are a hell of a lot sharper than mine) didn't have any inkling of trouble.

When the three-quarter moon had made about half its journey across the star filled sky, I woke Patch. He was still stiff and sore from his run-in with the outlaws. By the time I curled up into my bedroll, he seemed wide awake.

The whole damned thing lasted maybe three seconds for me. I awoke to Goldfire whinnying loud, with fear and panic in his voice. I was instantly awake. I pushed myself up on one arm to look around. There was an explosion in my head and the world went black.

*

Damn, I hate gettin' myself knocked out!

Not only because it tends to hurt like hell, but also because I hate that feeling when you come back around; that tingly all over feeling, along with the heavy fog muddlin' your brain.

When I came around I was lying on my side; the back of my head felt like it was on fire. The first thing I saw was a lake of blood. My blood! Okay, maybe it was more like a pool of blood, or maybe even a puddle…okay a small puddle; but it was my blood damn it, and it scared the hell out of me.

About then I realized that I couldn't hear nothin' due to a shrill ringing that filled my head; and that scared me even more.

"Patch! Sunny! I gotta help them!" Those thoughts galloped through my mind, but before I could talk myself into movin', the ringing swelled louder and louder and started to echoin' around in my head till I couldn't stand it. My eyes slid shut and I drifted away on the cool autumn breeze.

The next time I rejoined the living I was a little better prepared to stay. My head still hurt like blazes and there was still some blood, but the ringing in my head had quit. What the hell had happened? Where were Patch and Sunny?

Before movin' I took a minute to listen real hard. I heard the creek rushing down below in its bed. I heard the light breeze rustling the gold and orange leaves of the aspen trees we were camped under. I didn't hear any human or animal sounds. I slowly raised my head and had a peek around.

The campfire had been kicked and scattered. The fire was out, but red-hot coals still glowed here and there on the ground. There was enough moonlight that I could tell I was alone.

I slowly struggled to my feet, and proceeded to sway back and forth like a sapling in a thunderstorm. I dropped back down to my knees.

On the other side of the fire ring was the heavy wool blanket that Sunny had been wrapped in. She was gone. There was no sign of Patch either, and from where I knelt I could see where the horses had been tethered; it looked like they were missing too.

Stranded out in that country with no horse and no supplies, with fall quickly passin' and winter bearing down; it was as good as a death sentence.

After a couple minutes I tried the standin' thing again. This time I was able to stay on my feet, but I still swayed like a drunk.

I could feel the crease across the back of my head where the bullet had grazed me. Touching it hurt like hell and it still leaked a little bit.

The bastards had shot me and left me for dead. I'm not sure if I owe my life to bad aim or a trembling hand. Maybe the son of a bitch was laughin' and it threw him off just enough.

When my balance returned and I steadied up a might, I began to look for clues. In the moonlight I couldn't make any sense of the horse prints in the dirt, I'd have to wait for daylight to read them.

At the edge of the embankment dropping down to the creek I saw some scuffle and skid marks in the dirt. I looked over the edge and was just able to make out the black silhouette of a body layin' beside the rushing water twenty feet below me.

I scrambled over the edge and slid down the steep incline on my butt. When I got to the bottom I hurried to Patch's side. He was hurt bad, but he was breathin'.

I struggled back up the bank; got my bedroll and Sunny's blanket, and took them down. I cleaned out a couple of the biggest gashes on his head, and then covered him the best I could so he'd stay warm. There wasn't much else I could do till sunup. I didn't figure it'd be long in comin'; the black between the stars in the east looked a shade less black than to the west. I decided to take me a walk till daybreak.

By the time dawn had begun to light the eastern sky, our plight had improved considerably.

I'd hiked out into the plains above the campsite and there I found Goldfire with Patch's horse and both packhorses. Sunny's pony was gone. It looked like Chavez and his men had spooked the horses figuring they'd just keep runnin'. They hadn't counted on a horse as smart as Goldfire.

After bringing the horses back and tending to their needs I went to check on Patch.

When I looked over the embankment down to where the creek ran, Patch was sittin' up with one of the blankets wrapped around his shoulders. His head rested in the palms of his hands.

And then I was guilty of that "not thinkin' thing" again when I started scrambling down the incline before calling out first.

Patch heard the rocks start tumbling and he figured Chavez and his desperados had come back to finish the job. In a panic, he rolled over and sorta spider walked on all fours several feet downstream. Then he turned, squatted low to the ground, grabbed up a large rock in each hand, and prepared to lay down his life if need be, but determined to do some damage goin' out.

"It's me, Patch." I lost my footing and landed on my butt. "Only me."

"Damn it, Mount." Patch dropped the rocks. His hands went back to either side of his head. "You need to holler at a fella. I ain't doin' so hot right now anyway."

"Sorry Patch."

His hands came away and his head turned upward. I knew what was comin', and I wasn't looking forward to it.

"Sunny?" Patch's eyes filled with concern. "Is Sunny okay?"

"I don't rightly know, Patch." I could hardly get above a whisper.

"What the hell you mean, you don't know? Hell, Mount, either she's okay, or she's…"

"She's gone, Patch."

"No, Mount." Fear filled his voice and eyes. "No, don't say that. No. Maybe she's hurt and just wanderin' somewhere. Maybe?"

"Yeah, Patch." We both knew that wasn't the case. "Maybe."

*

"I'm gonna ask you to do me another favor, Mount."

It'd been quite a struggle for the two of us to make our way up the steep embankment, but somehow we done made it. I used my steel and built a fire. Patch sat and fed the flames and gathered his wits. I went and studied tracks. I'd just moseyed back to the fire and sat down.

"I'd like you to take my packhorse with you. I can't go chasin' Chavez and his bandits leadin' a damn packhorse." I'd already started shakin' my head. "I'll come for him as soon as I'm able." I continued to shake my head. "What the hell you mean, no?!"

"I mean I can't take your packhorse."

"Mount, I can't…"

"Because I ain't goin' home."

"You ain't goin'…"

"I ain't about to let you go after those no accounts all by your lonesome. Like it or not, I'm comin' along."

"Mount, I can't ask you to…"

"You ain't askin'. I'm telling you. You're stuck with me until we catch those varmints and get Sunny back. Hell, them sons-a-bitches shot me! Ain't nobody gettin' away with that!"

"Mount, I…"

This time I didn't interrupt him, he just had trouble talkin' for a bit.

"I didn't see who attacked us," I said. "but the tracks show four riders, so I'd bet my whole damn valley it was Chavez."

"I seen 'em." Now Patch's eyes blazed with pure hate. "I damn near got away when they tried to grab me. It was Chavez and his boys alright."

"Tracks head north, same direction we were goin'."

"Let's get packed up and get after 'em. Thank you, Mount."

We had to take the packhorses with us. They were going to slow us down considerable, but I couldn't leave a tethered horse, for God only knows how long, to fate. There were too many Indians, mountain men, trappers, settlers, and meat eating critters for a tethered horse to stand a chance.

It took but five minutes to bury the fire, and get our bedrolls tied in place. Patch carried Sunny's.

*

We rode hard; pushin' Patch's horse, and especially those packhorses, to their limit and beyond. Bein' early fall, it was a fairly cool day, but when I called our first halt, all four horses were lathered up and breathin' hard. I guess I was hoping we'd be able to run them bastards down in a hurry. That wasn't to be.

We rode all day. As we got closer to the mountains that had loomed in the distance, the territory got rougher and harder to travel, and the channel that the creek had slashed through the countryside got shallower. As soon as the creek and level ground joined up again the tracks we followed crossed the stream and headed northwest. When it got too dark to be sure of the tracks we reluctantly stopped for the night.

We took extra good care of our overworked horses and then built a fire.

"They don't have any reason to believe that we're trailin' 'em," I said. I was mostly thinkin' out loud as I stared into the fire. We were having a cold meal of jerked meat. "They figure we're both dead. So I'm betting they're travelin' slow and easy. We should catch 'em tomorrow, maybe the day after at the latest."

I looked over at Patch. He was starin' into the blaze same as me. The dancing flames lit his face, and shimmered off a tear rollin' down his cheek. He wiped it away angrily before looking at me.

"Damn it, Mount. I..." His lower lip began to tremblin' so hard his whole chin shook. He had to stare back into the fire for a spell before he could continue. "I've growed to like that...that little girl as if she was my own kin."

"She was a good kid, Patch." I realized what I'd said and corrected myself. If Patch had noticed he didn't show it. "She's a scrapper. I'm sure she's fine. We'll get her back in a day or two."

"That Chavez is a mean one, Mount." Patch's gaze stayed in the flames. I pretended not to see the tears that made their way down his creased, weathered cheeks. "There's no tellin' what them bastards are doin' to that poor girl."

"Well Patch." What does a feller say? "All I know is that frettin' about it ain't gonna help us or Sunny, and there's not a damn thing we can do until we catch up with them sidewinders. We ain't doin' Sunny a damn bit of good sittin' here imagining the worst."

"We need to catch 'em, Mount." Patch looked across the fire at me. He didn't even try to hide his tears. "We need to catch 'em fast."

We didn't.

We didn't catch them the next day; or the day after that. We came across a couple of campsites we figured were theirs, but couldn't be sure. The firestones were always cold as a December night.

Each of us leadin' a damn packhorse was slowing us down bad, but neither of us was willing to lose the animal or the valuable possessions they carried. If Chavez was hurryin' to get someplace, we didn't have a chance in hell of catchin' them. We just had to hope we'd catch up when they got wherever they was goin'.

And to make matters worse, we'd left the sandy prairie and had moved into the foothills with hard clay earth covered in tall grass; making tracking a whole lot harder. There were places where the tracks disappeared altogether and we had to guess which direction to go.

One of the five horses we followed had a double-split in its right rear hoof, so we always knew when we spotted the proper set of tracks.

It plumb amazes me that in a country with hundreds of thousands of square miles and only a handful of people, how there can be tracks and sign damn near everywhere.

We were still headed northwest and gaining elevation fast. The foothills changed from grass and sage covered to forest. Mostly pine, with a scattering of spruce, aspen, and oak.

Two dog-leg ranges of the Rockies had sprung up on either side of us. The mountains to the east were taller and more rugged. It was obvious that not too far ahead those two ridges were gonna meet.

My trips to and from Rendezvous had always taken me along the eastern edge of the Rockies, so Patch and I were in new territory to me. To both of us. Patch spending most of his time up in the north country.

Now, headin' through any Rocky Mountain pass (assuming there's gonna be one to go through) in the fall was not on the list of things I was hankerin' to do. We could already see fresh snow on the peaks, and you could bet yer gold mine that there was plenty more to come.

We spent our third night on the trail of those damned outlaws wrapped in our blankets and hunkered down beside the fire. We'd gained probably three thousand feet or so, and it was bone-chillin', death-dealin' cold after sundown. We positioned the fire so that we could lean back against an uprooted tree trunk; that way we were able to doze on and off while keepin' the fire stoked up. Patch had been real quiet like, mostly just staring off into the distance with a strange look in his eyes. A look that said when we caught up to Chavez and his men they were gonna regret the day.

Patch and I hadn't been on the move for but a couple hours the next morning when I smelled smoke.

"Smoke."

We pulled up. Patch tilted his head and flared his nostrils. Then he checked to see which way the breeze was coming from.

"Comin' from up the valley."

We backtracked into a dense portion of the forest and tethered the packhorses beside the creek where they had plenty of grass and water.

Mounted, but without the packhorses, the two of us were able to move quickly as we headed up the valley, staying under cover when possible.

It didn't take long and we came to a rock shelf. The smoke was rising into the sky from just beyond the edge. We tied off the horses; belly crawled to the rim, and peered over.

What a beautiful sight. There was a forty foot drop from the shelf where we lay to the ground below. In front of us, and spreading out east to west as it filled up the valley, was a large lake. Pretty much directly below us, at the outlet of the lake, stood an encampment of Indian teepees.

It was a small group. There were only eight teepees. From our hidin' spot we could see five squaws, three kids, and a couple of braves, all busy at some task or another. There were four meat-drying racks set up right below where the two of us lay; all four were full of strips of venison.

A twig snapped behind us. It didn't make no more noise than a grasshopper passin' gas, but Patch and I both heard it. As one we turned and looked back over our shoulders.

Three Indian braves stood twenty feet behind us. Their clothes and fixin's marked 'em as Salish Indians, usually friendly to the white man. All three of 'em had arrows notched and bows drawn back in a real unfriendly manner.

"Whoa, now hang on boys." Patch followed that up with a little bit of Indian jabberin'.

All my life in the mountains and I never learned more than a word or two of the Indian languages. Our rifles were primed and ready on the ground beside us, but there was no way we were gonna grab 'em and fire before gettin' poked. We slowly rolled over and sat up.

"We're friends of the Indians." Patch held his right arm out with his palm forward in the common gesture for peace or friend. We sure was countin' on those Indians knowin' that.

They didn't lower their bows, but they didn't shoot us either. The one in charge motioned for us to walk in front of them. One of the others picked up our rifles and we all strolled down and around the hillside and entered the camp from downstream.

A little Indian boy dressed against the cold in deerskins and knee high moccasins was the first to see us coming. He raised such a ruckus that within seconds Indians came scurryin' from all directions.

Those that brought us in kept us moving right through the camp to the last teepee. It sat off a piece from the others. An Indian elder sat before a fire ring cross-legged. In spite of the lively fire burning in the ring the Indian sat wrapped in a buffalo robe. It nearly matched Patch's.

The Indian stood as we approached. We stopped in front of him just as he threw back the hood that had covered his face. The old man was smiling.

"Well I'll be damned." Patch exclaimed beside me.

The aged gentleman stepped forward and extended his arm. Patch stepped forward and the two gripped each other's wrist. They jabbered back and forth for a few seconds.

"Mount, meet my old friend Chief Victor Grizzly Claw. Chief Victor, this is my friend, Mount."

We grasped wrists and the chief repeated my name. "Mount."

Patch continued on in English and with sign language for my benefit.

"Chief Victor, we look for four men and a young girl."

"Three men. No girl. Bad men." The elderly chief responded. "Dawn yesterday. They want meat. Have no trade. We tell go away."

"They probably kept Sunny hidden." I said.

"Where did the men go, Chief Victor?"

"Devil's Land." The chief pointed up the valley, beyond the lake. "Land of smoke. Land of stinking water. Devil's land."

Patch turned to me with a confused look. "I got no idea what in blazes he's talkin' about, Mount."

"I do."

Somewhere to the north of us, buried deep in the mountains, was Yellowstone Lake. The Yellowstone River is born there and starts its run down out of the mountains.

Now, the land directly around Yellowstone Lake is beautiful, and normal. Pa and I had been there one time, although we'd come down from the north. Magnificent mountain peaks. Rivers carving channels nearly a mile deep, down through steep-sided narrow gorges.

And as far as I know the water from Yellowstone Lake is as good and clean as any ice cold mountain water can be; nothin' bad in it except maybe a little elk or buffalo piss, and I've drunk plenty of both in my day.

If you wander west or southwest from the lake though, it don't take long till the land and the water get plenty strange.

The ground steams continually; as though there's a fire raging underground heatin' the water. The pools and streams are filled with hot water; boiling hot in some places, and the air stinks of sulfur. There are even spots where now and again the water will suddenly commence to shootin' outta the ground, up into the air a hundred and fifty feet or more.

Some Indian tribes think the land is blessed; the home of the gods. Others think the grounds are cursed and the abode of all sorts of evil spirits. Either way, no Indian in his right mind would voluntarily go into that odd country.

I sure as hell wasn't looking forward to it either because it's rough and dangerous territory, but if that's where Chavez took Sunny, then that's where we were headed.

Patch and Chief Victor spent a minute or two in conversation. When they broke apart the chief went to speak to the braves that'd brought us in. Patch hurried over to where I stood.

"The Chief's boys are gonna fetch our packhorses." He said. "They'll hold 'em for us till we get back."

"Hold 'em, or steal 'em?"

"Well, I guess that depends on how long till we get back. The Chief says they'll be here at least another week huntin' and fishin' to stock up for winter, then they'll be high-tailin' it down into the low country."

We'd already wasted too much time. After a quick word of thanks to Chief Victor, Patch and I hurried to where our horses waited. The chief himself rode out and showed us the trail of the varmints we was chasin'.

Chapter Five

We rode hard. And it hurt like hell. The bullet crease across the back of my head burned like blazes and my head throbbed every time one of Goldfire's hooves hit the ground. And I had it plumb easy compared to Patch.

Now, tough ole mountain man or not, gettin' beat up (again), and thrown down a steep embankment is hard on an elderly feller. Patch rode doubled over, his face nearly in the bay's mane. He held onto the reins with one hand and his ribs with the other. I could see the pain in his eyes, but the rest of his face barely showed it.

We had the lake on our left and real easy ridin' for the first couple hours, then we left the lake behind, and with it, the easy trail.

Dark kinda snuck up on us, as it tends to do in the mountains; especially in the fall of the year. As night settled down around us, we slowed to a walk while making our way up through a steep, rocky ravine. We'd made it past the steepest part and the ground leveled out some. It was still tricky goin' 'cause of the gigantic boulders and half rotted skeletons of dead trees that covered the bottom and sides of the gorge.

Since there wasn't anyplace worth a damn to stop for the night, and a nearly full moon lit the valley, we kept on the move; slowly picking our way up the treacherous ravine.

Twice the good Lord rewarded us with a clear set of prints in one of the few bare patches of dirt. In one of them we even saw the clear print of that double-split hoof.

Two or three hours before sunup the moon set and we were forced to stop. We'd cleared a high ridge and had started down into the next valley, so a few stands of live trees; the tougher pines, and some juniper bushes had begun to spring up. We stopped beside a big juniper, and used it as a wind-block for the cold breeze that was blowin'. We got as comfortable as possible and rested ourselves and our horseflesh till the first hint of light.

*

After a few bites of jerky and takin' care of morning business, we were in the saddle and movin' as soon as the horses could see their way.

Another several hours of ridin', most of it at a slow, careful walk, brought us to where the going finally got easier. And that fact alone saved our hides.

The mountain peaks still reared up several thousand feet on either side of us, but the valley floor, which would be filled with rushing water in the spring, had widened out and was covered in a green blanket of grass with willows lining the creek banks. The sky was a faded blue with just a few thin wispy clouds.

We stopped to water the horses, and ourselves, at a small spring. Remember folks, it's always a good idea to drink *upstream* from the horses.

There were clear and fairly fresh tracks. That double-split hoof was among 'em. We were still on the right trail, and it looked like we was finally gainin' some ground on the bastards.

It wasn't more than half an hour after we'd had our drinks at the spring that the damned mountain tried to fall on us.

A tremendous *CRACK* split the air. It was like a thousand thunder claps. Both horses froze in their tracks, flared their nostrils, and tested the air for trouble.

It was perfectly quiet for several seconds and then a low rumble began off in the distance, to our right. Our view in that direction was blocked by the pine trees that had replaced the boulders and sagebrush. The rumble quickly got louder.

"It's a rockslide!" I yelled. Goldfire began to dance and twist under me. He wanted to run.

"Which way?"

And that was the problem. That ominous crashing and grinding came from the east, but was it in front of us, or behind us?

You can't run from a rockslide until you know where the damn slide is. The rumble had become an earsplitting roar that filled the valley, and it was impossible to tell. The trees prevented us from seein'.

And then I saw a few small rocks bounce across our path. In the next instant a monstrous cloud of dust rose above the tree tops to our right.

"Back!" I didn't even tighten the rein on his neck and Goldfire spun around and took off like the wind; grateful for a direction and permission to run. "Follow us!" I managed to yell over my shoulder. And we were gone.

I stood in my stirrups, carrying my weight with my upper legs. Goldfire jumped left, then twisted right, and back left again, picking his route carefully, while still putting distance between us and the slide; and Patch and his bay mare.

The noise became deafening. The general roar was mixed with individual crashes as large boulders began bouncing and rolling into the ravine behind us. Smaller stones were bouncing across the trail in front of us.

"Run, Goldfire, run!" I was up off the saddle and leanin' forward as we climbed a gradual incline. I couldn't think about where Patch was; I could only urge Goldfire to run faster. The bay mare that Patch rode was a big strong horse, but I didn't know if she was gonna be fast enough? She didn't have to keep up with Goldfire; she only had to outrun that damned falling mountain.

It wasn't a big rockslide, as far as rockslides go. Hell, I've even seen bigger my own self (from a safe distance), but even a small rockslide will kill ya in an instant if you find yourself in front of one of those tumbling boulders.

I let Goldfire run till all sound of the slide stopped. At the top of a little knoll I reined him in. From a few hundred feet below where we stood the rest of the valley was hidden in a huge, boiling cloud of dirt, dust, and rock. There was no sign of Patch or his horse.

Goldfire and I rode back down until the cloud overtook us, but I couldn't see ten feet and couldn't breathe. I wasn't gonna be helping Patch any by ridin' down into that choking cloud.

We rode back up into clean air and I dismounted. As hard as it was to wait, that's just exactly what I had to do. It was all I *could* do.

It only took a minute or two for the biggest pieces to clear the air. Another couple of minutes and the cloud had settled out to a fine dust. I headed down to find Patch.

Part of me was afraid I wouldn't find him. Another part was nearly as afraid that I would.

*

It could've been worse; but it was plenty bad enough.

I saw the horse first. She was layin' quietly on her side, gasping for air. She'd given up. The foam lathered up around her mouth and the sweat running from her shoulders and haunches told me how hard she'd struggled to get to her feet. She could've tried until the stars burned out; she wasn't going to make it.

Both hind legs were broke bad. A saddle-sized chunk of granite was on the ground not far behind her. It was stained with blood and matted horsehair.

She'd almost made it. There were lots of smaller pieces of rock layin' around, but it was the very damned edge of the slide. If that mare would've had ten more steps she'd of been in the clear.

I primed my American "Trade" flintlock pistol and its .74 caliber ball ended her suffering.

From where I stood it looked like the slide stretched maybe five hundred feet down into the valley. The dirt, rocks, and boulders were piled up over twenty feet deep in places.

Just a couple feet from where the horse lay, there was a cabin sized boulder. It hadn't been part of the rockslide. Not that last one anyway.

And on the *other* side of that huge boulder lay Patch.

How the hell he ended up on the other side of that chunk of granite without gettin' smashed to bits is a mystery to me; and a miraculous, life saving blessing for Patch.

When I knelt down beside him, Patch's eyes were wide open, but not seein' a damned thing. He stared beyond me, beyond the clouds passin' overhead, beyond the sun itself.

So I did what any mountain man would do for another. I slapped him. Hard. Twice.

"Patch!" I didn't know where the next spring was, so I didn't want to waste any water. I slapped him again. "Patch! You in there?"

His eyes closed. I could see his eyeballs movin' around; I figured that was a good sign. It was.

When Patch opened his eyes the next time they were still dazed for a couple seconds, then they focused.

"Mount." He looked around, moving only his head. "What the hell...?"

"Rockslide."

"Oh yeah." I was mighty relieved that he seemed okay. "I thought we'd outrun it."

"You damn near did." I glanced down the valley to where the slide piled up. "One of the last good sized rocks got ya."

I saw a look of concern spread across Patch's face. He began struggling to get up.

"Sunny." It took a couple of tries for him to make it over to his hands and knees. "We need to get after Sunny, Mount." He planted his right foot, used both hands on his knee, and pushed himself upright. He groaned and I caught him as he started to fall over.

"Steady there, partner." I put him back on his own feet, but held onto his arm; as his balance returned, a new concern occurred to Patch.

"My horse," He looked me in the eye. "Is she...?"

"Yeah." There was no hidin' the truth. "Both of her hind legs were broke."

Patch took a couple of unsure steps, then sturdied up and managed to stagger around the boulder, using it for support.

He stood beside the dead mare. His head bowed and his eyes closed. He may've been praying.

He wiped angrily at his eyes and blew his nose out onto the ground as he squatted and began to undo his bedroll from the saddle.

"Thanks for takin' care of her, Mount." Patch stared straight ahead. "Always have hated puttin' a good animal down."

"It ain't never a pleasant chore."

"Well, I'll leave it up to you, Mount." Patch stood with his bed roll. "We can either go on ahead, or you can ride me back to Chief Victor's camp."

As Patch headed towards Goldfire I walked to the other side of the mare and started undoing the saddle.

"We'll go on." I said. "We can't afford to lose any more time." I threw the cinch over the carcass, stepped across and pulled the saddle free. "We'll hide your saddle and pick it up on the way back."

"Damned if you ain't an optimistic bastard, Mount." Patch was smiling and shakin' his head.

"You don't think we'll be comin' back?" I asked. Hell, I hadn't even thought of that possibility.

"Shoot," Patch rubbed his sore back. "If I know that Sunny is okay, and the swine that took her are feedin' worms...I'll be satisfied."

"Well, you don't mind if I go ahead and plan on livin' through this do you?"

"Suit yourself."

Chapter Six

Goldfire, that magnificent Palomino stallion, had become mine just past midway of our journey along the Oregon Trail, so it'd been nearly three years, and that horse still amazed me pretty much every day. Not only his intelligence, but his strength and stamina were a wonder to behold.

He could run uphill all day long without a problem, and do it faster than most horses goin' downhill.

That stallion had to climb up onto the mountainside thirty feet or more in some places to get around the jumbled remains of the rockslide. The slope was steep and covered with loose rock, sagebrush, and juniper bushes. That big Palomino traversed it all with two men on his back and returned us safely to the trail every danged time, as sure footed as a mountain goat.

"We gotta help that little girl, Mount." I could hear the tremble in Patch's voice. "Lord knows what those pigs are..." He didn't finish that thought. At least not out loud.

Patch sat behind me. Both his hands had a hold of my upper arms. Every time he got jolted or jostled, which was constantly, I'd hear him grunt from the pain and feel his hands clamp down on my arms. He was hurtin' bad.

It was as if Goldfire could sense our desperation, our feeling of foreboding; like he somehow knew that we were running out of time. After we made it around the slide area and back into the bottom of the ravine, he broke into a fast trot. A pace he could keep up for days if need be.

After a few miles we came to another steep incline that snaked its way up through a narrow, rock and brush filled coulee. We were forced down to a crawl as Goldfire picked his way through.

Once we maneuvered our way past that spot the valley opened up and widened out. Goldfire returned to his brisk trot, and the miles rolled away underneath us.

We camped out one more night. Around noon the following day we topped a knoll and a scene pretty enough to make your eyes hurt was spread out in front of us.

An enormous lake filled the valley as far as we could see. A narrow beach of rocks and sand bordered the near-side of the lake. From there a grassy meadow reached to the tree line. The meadow was filled with yellow, knee-high grass and late-blooming, high-country wildflowers.

The surrounding foothills were blanketed in either a green pine forest or short, brown sun burnt grass. Scattered about were blazing patches of orange, red, and gold where the aspens, oaks, and cedars prepared for winter. The hills continued on to rise up into majestic, snow covered mountain peaks.

From the size of it, the lake had to be Yellowstone Lake; the source of the great Yellowstone River.

As beautiful as the country was, we didn't take any time slowin' down to admire it. Neither of us could shake that feeling of anxiousness; or maybe it was just downright fear. Fear of what might be happening to Sunny.

Goldfire continued to sense it too and he never slowed his pace.

As near as we could tell, we were in the southeastern corner of the lake. It looked like we were maybe on the southern tip of an arm extending off from the main lake. Lookin' due north I could just make out where it appeared that the water opened up and spread out. Across to the west I could see land a mile and a half or so away.

As the afternoon rolled on we skirted the eastern edge of Yellowstone Lake headed north. The mountain peaks to our right, on the other side of the water, easily soared to over nine thousand feet.

Twice we spotted tracks along the lake's edge, and both times that double-split hoof was there, stamped in the mud plain as a pig's snout.

Getting on towards evening the weather commenced to changin'. What'd been a peaceful, clear blue sky turned a real serious lookin' light gray, and seemed to sink down right over our heads. The temperature dropped probably twenty degrees over the next couple of miles.

"Storm's fixin' to move in." Patch said from behind me. He pulled his buffalo robe tighter, makin' me wish to hell I had *my* buffalo robe. Mine was hangin' on a peg keepin' the wall warm inside my cabin. I'd been overloaded heading to Rendezvous, and besides, I never figured I'd be needin' it before I got home.

After another ten degree drop in the temperature I stopped and used some long, twisted blades of grass to fix a broken lace at the neck of my buckskin shirt, and to seal up the wrists. I had my rabbit-skin hat rolled up in my gear. I dug it out and pulled it down over my ears. With my neck and arms sealed and my ears covered, it was better, but still mighty cold. If it turned into a real nasty early-winter storm, I'd be in big trouble.

The only way to survive a bad storm would be to stop and build a fire and some sort of shelter. We didn't have time for either.

That's about when it started snowin'.

"We may need to stop and hole up, Mount." I could hear the reluctance in his voice. "You ain't dressed proper for a good ole mountain snowstorm."

"I'll be alright." I was damn cold, but not dangerously so. "As long as the wind don't blow I'll be able to keep going."

And about then the damned wind picked up.

I made it another mile. By then we were smack in the middle of a full-fledged blizzard. It was snowin' feet per hour, not inches, and the wind was howling down from the north and directly into our faces, makin' the temperature, which must'a been in the teens, feel a whole lot colder.

"I gotta stop!" I yelled back over my shoulder. I could just barely make out a large undercut along the bank of a creek we were passin'. It'd make a passable shelter out of the wind. With my fire-steel and some good luck, I might even be able to get a fire started; assuming we could find something dry enough to burn.

Patch didn't respond. He was buried so deep in his robe and under his coon skin hat that he couldn't hear me above the storm.

I was guiding Goldfire towards the creek bed when I smelled it...and then it was gone. I stopped and tested the air. It was near impossible gettin' a fix on anything in that snow-filled rush of wind. There it was again.

"You smell smoke?" I yelled. There was no response.

I threw a hard elbow behind me and was rewarded by a loud grunt. I felt Patch sit up.

"You smell smoke?"

I was just about to throw another elbow when he answered.

"Nope."

The word had barely cleared his mouth when I got another strong whiff.

"Yeah! Yeah, I smell somethin'."

"Me too." I nudged Goldfire on; my heart suddenly racing and my nerves on edge. I don't remember even feeling the cold anymore.

Within a hundred feet we were smelling smoke with every breath. I led Goldfire into a dense stand of pine that was to our right. It didn't help much, but it gave him some protection from the worst of the storm.

Now normally when you take off on foot in unfamiliar territory you'd take a gander around and pick out a couple good landmarks to guide you back.

That's damn hard to do when you can't see but twenty feet.

As it turned out we didn't have any need for landmarks. We hadn't gone fifty feet when Patch spotted a flame dancin' in the wind. He grabbed my arm and pointed.

We had to squint because of the wind and snow, but sure enough, just now and then, flashin' through the blizzard, I saw flames too. We primed our guns, dropped down onto our bellies and crawled. We were careful to carry our guns with a hand cupped over the flash-pan to keep the flint from gettin' wet and not sparking.

It was them.

Patch and I angled left as we belly-crawled closer. There was a patch of tall, sturdy weeds blowing in the wind and poking up above the snow, which had really begun to pile up. By the time we got into those weeds we could see down into Chavez's camp.

Actually, it was more of a burrow then a camp. There'd been a gigantic cottonwood tree uprooted. The enormous root system, standing on end like it was, made a solid wall nearly six feet high. There was a four foot deep hole in the ground where the roots had torn out.

Chavez, his three men, and Sunny were hunkered down in the hole, huddled around the fire. Sunny was in the near corner where the roots and dirt wall met. Her knees were drawn up to her chest and she was wrapped in a blanket. Her eyes stared at the ground in front of her. She looked half frozen and downright miserable, but she seemed to be unhurt.

Down in that hole like they were, with the root wall for protection, the fire burned, but barely. It danced and whipped around in the wind. It'd suddenly flare up and jump above the edge of their burrow, and then it'd die back down and look like it was about to sputter out any instant. There was no sign of their horses.

As we watched, we saw Chavez gesture angrily towards one of the men. He then pointed out in our direction. I figured he was ordering him to go get more firewood.

The feller shook his head disgustedly and gestured furiously at Sunny.

"Yeah, please send Sunny out for wood. She wouldn't dare run away in this storm," I thought to myself. Chavez wasn't havin' none of it.

Another angry gesture and the feller scrambled up out of the hole and headed straight towards the weeds where Patch and I lay. He was going for the pine forest behind us where all the dead branches were scattered around; and where my horse was waiting.

None of the five of them were geared up for winter weather either. The hombre fetchin' the wood, one of the white men, stopped when he got out in the wind, pulled his deerskin jacket tight around his shoulders, bent over into the wind, and preceded to walk less than ten feet beside us into the trees.

After breathin' sighs of relief, Patch and I crawled backwards until we felt safe, then got up and followed.

You don't need to try very hard to be quiet in the middle of a raging blizzard. Once we got in amongst the trees the force of the wind let up considerably and we were able to see further. The varmint we were following was only a few feet ahead of us; kicking the snow away and picking up branches. I could see the ghost shadow of Goldfire not too far in front of him, but he hadn't noticed yet.

I figured that I'd be the one to jump him when the time was right. I was younger, bigger, and stronger than Patch. None of that mattered a damn bit to Patch. I was just gettin' ready to step up and clobber the guy when that old mountain man took two running steps and a jump and landed square in the middle of that feller's back.

A grunt of surprise escaped from him as Patch rode him to the ground. I expected the grunt to be followed by a call for help. I'm not sure if it would've carried through the storm back to the others or not. We didn't find out because the varmint never got the chance to yell.

I hadn't seen Patch pull the large skinning knife from its sheath on his belt. When I stepped up, ready to help keep the man quiet, Patch rose and sat back on his haunches. His knife was buried to the hilt in the sidewinder's throat. As we watched, that outlaw's life-blood pumped out into the snow, and his open, fear-filled eyes glazed over with the see-nothin' stare of death.

Patch reclaimed his knife, used a handful of dirt and pine needles to wipe it off, and without a word to each other we turned and headed back.

While we were still hidden from view by the storm, I signaled to Patch that I'd circle left. He nodded, dropped down to his hands and knees and started crawling forward.

I looped around, crossed over, and came back along the trunk of that huge cottonwood whose roots the gang hid behind. I was still too far away to help when Patch made his move. If he would've waited even another damned few seconds, things may've turned out different. But he didn't.

I was crouched over makin' my way through the branches that still stuck out from the dead trunk of that giant tree when I heard a wild Indian war-cry cut through the howling wind and blowing snow. I started runnin'. I'd only taken a step when I heard a gunshot and more screaming. I got to that vertical wall of roots and dirt about the time I heard a second shot.

Grabbing hold of a large, thick root I used it to swing myself around and down into the hole. Before I even landed, I surveyed the scene in front of me. One body lay on the ground at the outside edge of the burrow. Patch was on the ground too with his head and shoulders over the edge of the hole. He was trying to aim his handgun, but seemed to be having trouble.

Directly in front of me was the last of Chavez's henchmen; the Mexican. He stood facing Patch, with his back to me. Chavez stood off to the right, also looking towards where Patch lay. Chavez had a gun in his hands. Sunny was curled up on the ground, pressed up against the tree roots.

I hadn't pulled my gun because I figured it'd be too close quarters for shootin'. As my boots hit the ground the feller in front of me started to turn. I slammed my left forearm against the base of his neck and used my huge right fist to wallop him up alongside the head with everything I could muster. Even over the shrieking storm I heard his neck snap.

Chavez was turning towards me and raising his gun. One step and I was within reach. My right hand shoved the gun away while my left hand locked onto the bastard's throat; prepared to choke the life out of him. I slammed him back against the root wall.

He hadn't dropped the gun, and it was swinging around to point at the side of my head. I was forced to release my grip on his throat.

With both hands I grabbed his gun hand and twisted. The shootin' iron went off directly into the tangle of roots. Dirt, mud, and branches exploded beside my face. Suddenly my ears were ringin' and my eyes were full of grit. I was fightin' blind. I tried to blink my eyes clear, but there was just too much dirt.

I shook his wrist like a mad dog with a snake, and felt the gun fly from his grip. Then I wrapped my arms around him and rode him to the ground. I needed to control him so I could use at least one hand to clear my eyes.

Chavez didn't exactly see things my way. He commenced to fightin' like a wounded grizzly sow with a cub.

I still had one of his arms trapped, but the other had pulled free and began to poundin' on the side of my head. I used my weight advantage to pin him to the ground, pulled my left arm free and tried to corral the arm that was pummeling me.

I tried to force my eyes open, but all I saw was dirt and tears. I squeezed them shut again. The pain was like glowing embers from the fire had burrowed into both eyes.

I rose up a little to gain some leverage. I sat astride him at about the stomach. He was twistin' around like a buckin' bronc, but he couldn't throw me.

I still had one arm pinned. The other was still beatin' the hell out of me. Getting a grip on that arm was like tryin' to grab a fish underwater. I'd grab and miss and he'd clobber me in the head. I'd grab again. His arm would slip away and he'd hit me again. My head was ringin' like a church bell.

Without being able to see, there wasn't much else I could do. I needed to keep him pinned to the ground; but damned if I could control that fist that kept wailin' on my head. I was startin' to get dizzy and sparkly lights began flashin' and dancin' on the backs of my eyelids.

And then it was over.

The fist that was pounding me suddenly stopped. I felt Chavez's body tighten for a second and then relax.

What the hell? He hadn't given up; I knew better than that. Was he playin' possum? Waiting for me to let up so he could renew his attack? I held him tight for a few more seconds. Nothing happened.

Finally, the pain in my eyes forced me to decide. I let go and rolled hard to my right. I rolled twice to make sure I had some room. My body slammed up against the side of the hole. Both hands came up to frantically wipe mud from my eyes as I scrambled to my feet. My gut was tensed up as I expected to be knifed or shot at any instant. It didn't happen.

By the time I got my eyes clear enough that I could begin to see some, I'd already figured out that the fight was over. I wasn't sure what'd happened, but I knew that if Chavez was comin' he'd have already been there. I wiped and blinked, wiped and blinked, and did it again before I could finally focus on the damned bloody mess around me.

The white man was dead at the front of the burrow. Part of the feller's forehead was missin' from where Patch had shot him from close range.

The Mexican I'd surprised was dead at my feet with his head resting at a strange angle.

Patch laid where I last seen him, half in and half out of the hole. He wasn't movin'.

Directly in front of me Chavez was still on his back, the handle of a large knife stickin' outta his bloody chest; just about where his heart would've been, if he'd had one.

Sunny was on her knees beside his body staring down at him. Her eyes filled with anger and hate, and a good measure of fear and shock. Tears rolled down her cheeks. Her right hand was covered with blood.

She saw me move and turned her head in my direction.

"I killed him, Mount."

It was then that I noticed the wind had quit blowin'. I noticed because she had whispered, and I'd heard her. It was still snowing heavily, but there was no more wind.

"I killed him." She repeated. There was disbelief in her voice.

Killin' a man, even a no-account snake like Chavez who deserves it, is a hard thing. It's a hard thing for a grown up man, let alone a young woman.

Not knowin' what to say, I didn't say anything. I stepped around the bodies on the ground and went to check on Patch. Just as I got to him there was a loud shriek behind me that nearly scared me clear to death. Before I could get spun around Sunny was beside me, reaching out to Patch.

"Patch!" She was crying. "Oh God, Patch don't be dead. Please don't be dead."

And he wasn't. Not quite.

I climbed out of the hole and knelt beside him. Slowly and gently I rolled him onto his back. I leaned over him to keep the snow from falling in his face. His eyes fluttered but stayed closed, a groan escaped his lips. His buffalo robe had opened and revealed an ugly hole in his chest.

Blood bubbles leaked from the wound. That told me that he was breathin'. It also told me that he was hurt real bad; a lung had been punctured.

Sunny stood with her feet still in the burrow and her right arm across Patch's body; just below the injury. Her left hand stroked his coonskin hat as though petting a dog. Tears rolled down both her cheeks.

Another groan and Patch's eyes quivered and then opened. It took him a few seconds before he was able to focus. A small, pained smile bent his lips when he saw Sunny's tear streaked face hovering over his.

"You...you're okay?"

"Yeah, Patch." Sunny laughed through her tears. "Yeah, thanks to you, I'm okay."

He turned his head to me. I saw the question in his eyes; there was no need for words.

"Chavez is dead, Patch." I was havin' a hard time talking myself. I had to take a deep breath before going on. "All four of them sidewinders are dead."

His eyes shifted from me to Sunny and back again.

"Take care of..." It was all he could manage.

"I will, Patch." I guess there was still some dirt in my eyes because they was waterin' real bad. "I will."

"No! No, Patch!"

Patch somehow found the strength to raise his arm. He took Sunny's hand in a feeble grip and smiled a weak smile. A tear escaped from his right eye, rolled over his cheek, and disappeared into his beard. His eyes slowly closed and Patch Willis took his last breath.

"No...no...no...no." Sunny's voice faded away as she buried her face in Patch's neck. Her shoulders shook as she sobbed.

Now, the mountain man way of life is a hard one, and death ain't never far away; but knowin' that don't make it any easier to lose a good friend.

Patch had had a good life. He'd lived longer than most folks get a chance to, and knowin' that didn't make it a damn bit easier either. He was a mighty good man and I'm gonna miss him.

*

I left Sunny to mourn while I went lookin' for the five horses that I knew had to be close by. At some point during the storm and all the ruckus, daylight had slipped away and night had taken its place. Suddenly I was aware of the cold again; it was damn cold.

The snow had let up. Just a few flakes drifted lazily down through the night sky. There was five or six inches of fresh snow covering the ground with eight to ten foot drifts in the places where the wind had piled it up. There were no stars or moon to be seen, but there was enough reflection off the new blanket of snow, that I could see fairly well.

I found the horses in a small stand of aspen trees down towards the lake. Those dumb bastards had tied those critter's reins to tree branches so those poor animals couldn't move or even lower their heads enough to forage for grass. All five stood bunched up with their heads hangin' low.

I untied each one, tethered their legs so they wouldn't run off, and hurried back to Sunny. The horses had burrowed through the snow and were eating before I was out of sight.

When I got back Sunny was sitting up beside Patch's body. Her arms were wrapped around herself and her whole body shivered; and not from crying, although she still did.

The Mexican, whose neck I'd broke, wore a heavy wool coat. I worked it off him and wrapped it around Sunny.

"No!" Despite the cold, she tried to push it away.

"Yes." It was no time to be stubborn. "It's a coat. It ain't evil, it's just warm." I laid it over her shoulders and held it there. It didn't take but a couple seconds for her to change her mind. She put her arms through the sleeves and pulled the coat tight.

I had to fight different feelings towards Patch's buffalo robe. He sure as hell didn't need it anymore, and I needed it bad. I knew he'd tell me I'd be a damned fool not to take it, if he was able, but I still fought feelings of guilt as I wrestled the heavy garment off his body. Sunny looked like she wanted to say something when she first noticed, but she didn't.

I figure the warmth that spread through me like melted butter as I donned that buffalo skin was a much appreciated farewell gift from my old friend.

*

I didn't have any idea how long till daylight. I decided we'd stay put.

I was amazed to see that through all the fightin' and dying that'd been done in that hole, the fire hadn't been disturbed. The flames had long since gone out, and most of the coals were soaked and cold from the snow, but there were still a few glowing embers.

The first thing I did was fetch our horses. I rolled Patch's body up inside his blanket, and then laid him down back away from the rim so we didn't have to see him.

Then I packed the three other dead bodies off into the trees and spread them around near where their other friend lay. Maybe a couple of grizzlies would wander by lookin' to fatten up for the coming winter.

With some dry moss, fine wood shavings, and dead branches I busted off of some tree trunks, it didn't take long to have a warming fire burning. I tethered the horses and brought our blankets. Sunny didn't like the idea of gettin' back in that hole but the cold night and the warm blaze brought her around. We sat side by side staring into the fire. Each of us lost in our own thoughts and a world of dancing flames.

At the first hint of light we set to work. The first task was giving Patch a proper burial.

After dousing the fire I gently laid his blanket-wrapped body in the hole. I put him in as tight up against the roots as I could. Beating and shaking that root wall got him mostly covered with dirt. And then we started haulin' rock.

No way in hell was I lettin' some critter gnaw on Patch. I would've hauled rocks for miles if needed. Luckily they weren't that far.

Less than a quarter mile to the west there was one of those tree-bare hills. It'd been the sight of a rockslide hundreds of years ago, and was covered with small boulders. I rigged a travois behind Goldfire using blankets and some pine branches.

We made six trips before I was satisfied. Despite the cold, Sunny and I were both leakin' sweat by the time we finished up.

"He was a good man." Sunny said. We were standing on the edge of what was now Patch Willis' grave. Sunny didn't try to hide her tears as she spoke. "He knew...up north before we left, he knew there'd be more trouble with Chavez." She wiped her cheeks and runny nose with her sleeve. "I was nothin' to him. Just a homeless kid." She laughed through her tears. "A wiseass kid at that." Sunny looked up into my eyes. "He didn't need to take me along, Mount. There was no reason for him to take me and my problems on." She turned back to the grave. "No reason, except that he was a good, caring man."

"And he had a good life." Mountain men don't usually cry; or at least don't usually own up to it, but I'll admit to sheddin' a couple tears for Patch Willis. Unlike Sunny, I tried to cover mine up. I wiped my face with both hands from top to bottom, and coughed awkwardly to get rid of the tremble in my voice. "He lived the life that he chose. He was free as a man can possibly be, and you can't ask for more than that." I put a comforting hand on Sunny's shoulder. "And he told me several times that he'd grown mighty fond of you, young lady."

She smiled, and happiness shone in her eyes, through the tears.

"You know how to pray?" she asked.

"Uh...do you?"

"Ain't ever tried."

"I pray all the time, sorta...in my head. Don't know that I've done it out loud since I was a young boy and knelt beside Ma at bedtime."

"Makes you more qualified than me. Go on now, Mount."

Sunny took my hand, closed her eyes, and bowed her head. I kept my eyes open and looked to the heavens. The clouds had begun to break up. The hint of light in the east had spread to become a promise of a beautiful fall day.

"Lord, we place before you a good man; Mr. Daniel Patch Willis. And Lord we wou..." Sunny's laughter interrupted me. I looked down as she glanced up.

"Daniel?"

"Yep, Daniel. I ain't ever heard anyone use it, but that's what it was. Ain't even sure why I know."

Her laughter faded away. I figured she just might laugh herself to death if she found out my handle was Thadius Beauregard Battner. I decided then and there not to tell her.

"Keep going, Mount."

"Lord, we'd appreciate it if you would accept Patch's spirit up there in Heaven. He was a good man, and deserves the best you got to offer. Thank you, Lord. Amen."

"Amen."

And with that, it was time to get the hell out of those mountains before the next blizzard moved in.

Chapter Seven

I had two choices. If we continued north, we'd eventually find where the mighty Yellowstone River drained out of Yellowstone Lake and began it's nearly seven hundred mile journey out of the mountains and across the plains to empty into the Missouri River.

And I figured that roughly halfway through the Yellowstone's run, near the border between the mountains and the plains, in a beautiful meadow beside a dancing creek, sat my cabin. A place I dearly wanted to get back to.

Our second alternative was to double back the way we'd come and head home by skirting the east side of the mountains, following the route I'd taken to Rendezvous.

I was tempted to continue on north just because it would've covered some new country for me, but I was pretty sure that it would've also been a longer trip.

I didn't know what that bitch, Mother Nature, had in store for us, and I still had hopes of claiming my packhorse and goods that we'd left with Chief Grizzly Claw.

We headed back the way we'd come.

We were lucky. I guess that blizzard we'd had was just a friendly reminder that winter was on its way, and not an indication that winter had arrived. The sky remained crystal clear and a blue so pretty it hurt your eyes. And the temperature was as warm as can be expected that time of year. We kept our coats on most of the time, and built a big fire in the evenings.

It was in front of one of those fires that I got up the nerve to ask Sunny about her ordeal.

She was wrapped up with the collar of her coat turned up, and her heavy wool blanket on top of that. She sat and stared into the fire with a strange, faraway expression.

"So, uh." It wasn't like I'd had a heap of experience talkin' with young ladies about such things. It was a first for this ole mountain man.

"Yeah, Mount?"

"So, uh," I looked into the fire. "I, uh, I was wonderin' if uh…"

"What, Mount?"

"Chavez, uh, and his men. Uh, I wondered, uh did they, I mean…"

I didn't know what sort of reaction I expected, but it sure as hell wasn't the one I got. Sunny's face brightened, and her mouth spread in a huge grin. She actually managed a small laugh.

"Thank you for asking, Mount. That had to've been hard for you." I gave her an embarrassed grin. "I was so scared when they grabbed me." Her face changed again, the fear she'd felt was reflected in it. "I didn't know if Patch and you were alive or dead. I was so scared of what they were going to do." The smile returned to her face. "Turned out they didn't do nothin'. Chavez wouldn't let the others touch me. I guess he wanted me for himself, and he must've been waiting till we got where we were going. I think he somehow suspected you and Patch were followin', because he seemed in one all-fired hurry."

"So, nothing, uh, I mean they didn't, uh?"

"No, Mount, they didn't. One night, after everyone else was asleep, Tom, the tall, skinny one, tried. I punched him in the nose, and kneed him, you know, down there, and he left me alone."

Much to my relief we never talked about it again.

*

It was tough makin' good time while leading four horses. When we got to the narrow and steep sections, we slowed to a crawl.

Makin' our way over and around the rockslide that had killed Patch's horse was probably the hardest part of the trip. I thought we was gonna have some more broke legs, but somehow we made it without having to shoot any horses. I stopped and picked up Patch's saddle.

It looked like the carcass of that big mare had fed several critters, at least one of 'em being a large bear. What was left stunk to high heaven.

Around mid-afternoon of the third day, we cleared a tree covered knoll and saw the lower lake; the one where Chief Victor Grizzly Claw and his people had been camped beside. We hurried around the western side of the lake; the going was much easier there in the lower country, along the grassy shore.

If we wouldn't have made it that day, we'd have missed Chief Victor and his people. When we rode into their camp that evening, everyone was busy. They were packing and loading the jerked and dried meat that they'd made, along with what belongings that they could, and preparing everything that could be made ready.

In the morning they'd tear down the teepees, tie the poles and hides to the packhorses and travois and be on their way into the prairie and south to their winter home.

I sat with Chief Victor, and using what Indian sign language that I knew, along with the little bit of English that he knew, plus plenty of gesturing and pointing, we had us a powwow. The chief appeared to be truly sorry to find out that Patch had died. He didn't seem to remember any packhorses loaded with supplies that we'd left with them. I didn't figure he would.

I'd left the four horses we'd been leadin' hidden back up the trail a ways just for such a situation. Chief Victor's eyes lit up when I led those four good looking saddle horses into camp; and damned if his memory didn't miraculously come back.

I ended up with my own packhorse and almost all of my supplies. I got all the main staples back anyway, the salt, flour, coffee and that sort of thing. I'd traded for a couple of real nice cast-iron cookin' pots down at Rendezvous, but none of the Indian women could seem to remember where they'd been packed away.

It was while I was trying to convince two of those ladies to look again, that I realized I hadn't seen Sunny for some time. I went lookin' and found her behind the camp by the makeshift corral. She was with another young lady about her own age. They were brushing what I guessed was the Indian girl's pony.

As I watched, along with the two elderly Indian women, the pony reached out and nuzzled Sunny's cheek, and then, as horses tend to do, it tried to bite her shoulder. Sunny pulled back in time, and the Indian gal gave the pony a playful swat on the nose. The horse drew back and shook its head back and forth. The two girls burst into laughter. I'm talkin' the holdin' your gut and shakin' your shoulders kinda laugh.

And I realized that that was the first time I'd ever heard her laugh like that. Even when Patch and I were at our best around the campfire she hadn't laughed like that.

And with a little whiskey in us, most of our stories were damn funny too; in fact some were plumb fall on your ass hilarious. I know that because both Patch and I *did* several times. And Sunny had laughed too, but not with the enthusiasm that she had with that Indian girl.

Now, I ain't never put much faith in what they call destiny; the idea that I ain't makin' up my own mind, but just followin' some sort of pre-planned life? Whether it be God himself doin' the plannin' or not, well, that just doesn't sit right down deep in my gut. And judging by some of the strange happenings in my life, well, there just ain't no way that somebody, somewhere had already thought of and planned that shit out.

Now in Sunny's case, I believe I'd have to make an exception. I truly believe that that half-breed Indian girl was meant to join up with Chief Victor Grizzly Claw and his group.

The old woman that stood beside me looked up into my eyes. I looked down into hers, and as easy as a nod of the head the decision was made. Sunny was welcome to stay.

I headed towards the girls. They saw me coming. The Indian girl smiled up at me, then lowered her eyes to the ground and walked away. Once she got past me, she broke into a run and ended up in the arms of the old Indian woman.

As I approached her, Sunny too stared at the ground.

"What's her name?"

"Spring? Maybe. Or Springtime? I ain't real sure."

"She seems nice."

Sunny looked up, her eyes so full of excitement that they twinkled like stars. "Oh, she *was*, Mount. She's real nice. She doesn't even seem to care that I'm a half-breed."

"Sunny and Spring. Sounds like a song and dance team down at Fort Granger." I gestured to where the woman and her daughter stood. "The old woman invited you to stay."

I swear that girl's whole body jumped as though she'd been stung in the butt by a hornet. I was afraid her lips were gonna split wide open, her grin stretched so wide.

"Really! They want me to..." I'm not sure what she saw in my ugly ole face, but she suddenly stopped. Her face grew solemn, and her gaze returned to the ground. "Oh, I don't know, Mount." She mumbled.

Now, I wanted Sunny to stay with those Indians, I truly did. I knew it was the best thing for her and me. She'd be far better off with them, and I'd sure as hell be better off without a damn kid worryin' me; but...those last few days on the trail, I'd kinda gotten used to the little smart-mouthed brat bein' around. She was good company. I was gonna miss the little troublemaker, and maybe that's what she saw in my eyes.

Well, despite any inclinations I might've had to the contrary, there was no debate about what needed to happen.

"I think it's a good idea. You stayin' with the Indians, that is."

"You do?" And the shine was back in her eyes, the grin back on her face.

"Well, I was really lookin' forward to having myself a little slave girl. You know, someone to do all the cookin' and cleanin' and…"

Suddenly my arms were full of giggling girl. We'd figured Sunny to be around twenty, making her a grown woman, but the bundle of excitement that was huggin' me that evening, acted about thirteen; and as excited as Christmas mornin'.

I spent the night. I was welcome to stay, but no one offered room in their teepee. Wrapped in the buffalo robe and my blanket, I slept fitfully beside the main campfire.

At first light, as if by some signal, the camp was suddenly alive and hard at work. With very little talking everyone went about their tasks. Campfires were extinguished completely. Teepees began coming down. Horses and travois prepared.

And Sunny and I said our goodbyes.

Sunny cried. And damned if I didn't get a gnat or some other flyin' pest in my eye; danged thing hit me so hard that both eyes watered up.

There were some tears, but we knew it was what needed to happen; the best for both of us. So the tears soon dried up. There was one final hug. Then I was surprised by a hug from Sunny's new "mother"; one that very nearly cracked a rib or two.

And a couple minutes later, just as I was mounting up, she came back carryin' one of my good, new pots. Seems she'd suddenly remembered where it'd been put. I thanked her and rode out of camp.

*

I was able to travel fast after leaving Sunny and the Indian camp; our only limitation was the stamina of my packhorse. It wasn't long before we dropped down off the mountain plateau where the lake was. A few hours later the mountains fell away and we were back in the flat land. I turned to the east until I cleared the lower leg of the mountain range, and then headed north and northwest towards home.

It took me three days to make the day and a half ride back to my cabin.

The afternoon of that first day, after leavin' Sunny with the Salish Indians, I rode up on eight head of mule deer. It was one big ole buck and his harem of seven fine lookin' ladies. That buck was in full rut, which meant it was getting later in the fall than I'd figured.

It also meant that ole buck had only one thing on his mind, and it wasn't me and Goldfire moseyin' by. He was dumber than an earthworm.

That big ole boy gave us an uninterested glance and pushed his ladies a couple hundred feet up onto the hillside before he stopped and began to bothering the girls around in circles.

I rode past till we were out of sight, tethered the horses, and put the stalk on the deer. I picked one of the smaller does. She wasn't big, but she was heavy after a long summer, and made for real good eating. I lost the rest of that day butchering and jerking deer meat.

And I could've made it home the next day except a faint whiff of sulfur reminded me of the hot springs that were hidden in the foothills not far away, and that I was stiff and sore clear to the bone from travelin'. I turned Goldfire to the east and headed for the hotpots and a medicinal soak.

There was a large creek moving a goodly amount of water, especially for that late in the year that snaked its way down out of the mountains. I suppose it dumps into the Yellowstone somewhere downstream.

Fifty feet on the west side of that creek is a sandstone cliff that rises in steps and shelves to around a hundred feet. Starting about halfway down the cliff, and for several shelves below that, hot water pours through cracks in the rock and fills a fairly large pool before running out and joining with the ice cold creek water.

That hot water felt so good on my trail-weary body that I changed my plan again and spent the night.

It was still early the next morning when we got to the Yellowstone River. All we had left was a couple miles upstream to where Sweetgrass Creek emptied into the Yellowstone, then upstream along the creek for another two miles or so and we'd be home. Even that tuckered out packhorse seemed to sense it and found a little extra get up and go.

And I was happy as a hungry bear at a crowded fishin' hole most of those last couple of miles too. I don't care how much traveling you do, there's just something good about gettin' home; knowing every bend in the creek, every tree, and every boulder. Hell even the weeds looked familiar.

The early mornin' frost was just starting to melt off the places where the sun had touched and still glistened in the shady spots.

Although my heart still ached over the loss of my friend, Patch, and I still fretted some over Sunny, it felt mighty good followin' that creek upstream and home.

And then, as I rounded one of those bends in the creek that I knew so well, a light breeze met me. It carried the unmistakable smell of smoke.

The grin left my face. I let the lead rope to the packhorse drop, and Goldfire took off. I don't think I even nudged him; we was just suddenly in a full gallop; the smell of smoke gettin' stronger with each step.

We came fast and tight around the three big cottonwood trees that were the last barrier blocking my view of the cabin. I reined Goldfire to a stop.

Most of my fear disappeared when I saw that the smoke came from my cabin's chimney. The fear faded and my curiosity peaked. Who would be stayin' in my cabin? Could I assume they were friends?

From the distance all I was sure of was three horses. It didn't look like they were saddled or had gear. That, plus the fire, told me that whoever it was had been there awhile.

Instead of ridin' directly up to the front door, I hugged the creek and stayed amongst the trees and behind the willows when I could.

I didn't have to get too much closer before I recognized the big bronze Quarter Horse and the stout Morgan packhorse. They belonged to another mountain man friend. Buck Nealy.

Buck had nearly drowned me when I was young. Because Buck had been the only person my folks knew that could sorta swim, they decided he was the one who needed to teach me how.

Buck's method was pretty damn simple; throw him in...he'll figure it out.

I damn near drowned, but it turned out that Buck was right in the end, 'cause I taught myself to swim after that. Not very good, but I can keep myself afloat.

I still didn't know who else was in my cabin. From where I was, Buck's two horses blocked my view of the third one.

I'd gone as far as I could along the creek. There was nothing left to do but ride out into the open. After recognizing Buck's horses I was confident that there wasn't gonna be any trouble.

I approached the cabin and the horses from the side. As Goldfire and I moved up on 'em, Buck's two became a little skittish, and stepped back. The third horse came into view.

Suddenly my heart was racing; poundin' like a buffalo stampede. I couldn't think, as a million different thoughts thundered through my head.

There stood Skyhawk. The spotted Mustang pony I'd owned before Goldfire.

I'd given Skyhawk to Andy; the teenage son of Mr. Andrew Worthington the Second and his wife, Sandra. The family I'd guided from St. Louis across the country to Oregon City. Andy and I had become like father and son during that cross-country trek.

I was debating whether to hurry back and get my packhorse or go in when the decision was made for me. The cabin door flew open and Andy came running out. At least I had to figure it was Andy. He sort of resembled the kid I'd known only two years before, but the boy was now a young man; a damn tall young man.

"Mount!" He stood on the other side of the hitchin' pole. Buck Nealy stood behind him in the doorway, grinin' like he'd struck gold.

I jumped off Goldfire as if he was on fire. I didn't make it to the post before nearly gettin' knocked over by that charging young man. Andy's arms squeezed me tight, like he didn't mean to let go. Not only had he growed, but that boy had gotten a lot stronger too. A sob escaped from his chest as he buried his face in my shoulder.

And I knew that it was more than just a friendly visit.

When he finally did let go and stepped back he had tears running down both cheeks. I noticed them as soon as I was done wiping my eyes clear. His tears curled around the corners of his mouth, as it was turned up in a big country grin, and then disappeared into a couple weeks' worth of beard.

I noticed that Buck had wandered back inside the cabin.

"Hi." He laughed. It was the best sound I'd heard in a long, long time.

"Andy…" I had to swallow a couple times before I could go on. "Damn boy, you've growed up. You ain't a boy no more."

"Yeah, look at me," He stepped back. "almost seventeen, six foot two and maybe still growing. I'll never catch you though, Mount."

"Damn well better not! I ain't accustomed to lookin' up at folks." I figured that was enough shootin' the breeze till later. Andy must've seen it in my face, because his got real serious looking too. "What you doing here, Andy?"

He looked down at the ground. "Its mom…well, I guess its father, because…well, mom is so scared and…oh gosh, Mount, it's hard."

Andy stood with his hands twisted together and his weight shifted from one foot to the other. He looked like he was fixin' to run away at any moment, and I'd never see him again.

I stepped up and put my arm across his shoulders and patted him on the back.

"I've got me a packhorse to fetch down the creek a piece, Andy. Let's take a ride. We can talk on the way."

"Yeah, okay Mount."

I expected him to ride behind me since Skyhawk wasn't saddled. He surprised me. Andy hopped up on that pony and rode bareback like he'd been raised up by the Apache. He used only the lead rope as his rein. He'd become a damn good horseman. We went along side by side at a plodding walk.

"Father's business venture failed, Mount. I guess everything started there." He began.

"Well, I don't know buffalo chips about business matters, but I can't see Mr. Andrew Worthington the Second making a bad business decision."

"Oh, he didn't, not really." Andy laughed without much humor. "It was a good business plan, but it was the wrong time and with the wrong partner."

"I reckon I still don't understand."

"It's simple, Mount." Once we'd got on horseback and commenced to movin' Andy's nerves settled right down and he was calm as a summer day. "Father had invested all of his money, and a considerable amount of other peoples', in the Oregon City endeavor. He received a huge shipment of goods which he had pre-paid for. He bought a building there on the main street of Oregon City, and set up a nice big store. The building and land was all financed on paper." Andy glanced up. "Then two things happened. First, instead of the steady growth in population that father had expected, and depended on, the population actually began to decrease. Some of the folks decided they weren't cut out for life out west, and headed back east. The more adventurous ones went north or south to homestead." Andy looked over at me. "The mass migration out west is going to happen eventually, maybe even within the next few years, but it didn't happen soon enough to save father."

"There was that sawmill just north of town."

"On Mill Island. Yeah, it's still there, but demand is low and they're working a skeleton crew." Andy answered. "There's even been talk of a milling company building down on Abernathy Island, but who knows?"

"You said two things happened?"

"The second was Mr. Brocknell, father's so-called business partner."

"Only person I ever met that was more high-brow than your Pa."

"Yeah, well it turned out that he was also disloyal and dishonest, Mount. Brocknell was the representative of the big money men back east. When he saw things were going to get tough, he cut and ran." Andy scratched Skyhawk between the ears absentmindedly as we rode. "Not only did he take most of the cash on hand, but when father tried to draw on the accounts back east, he found that they'd been cleaned out."

Andy laughed; with a touch more humor this time. "And, believe it or not, Mount, father ruffled some feathers around town. And mos…"

"No! Andrew Worthington the Second makin' folks mad? I'll be damned."

"So, most of the local people that were left in town continued to buy their supplies from the General Store. As things went from bad to worse father started drinking more and more. When word of that got around, the handful of folks that had shopped his store quit. Father was eventually forced to close the store, and couldn't make the payments on the building. His entire inventory is stored in the building. Mr. Jennings, owner of the General Store, holds the paperwork and gets a percentage of the inventory for each month father can't pay. He'll soon own it all, the goods and the building."

Now, that was all interesting enough, but I had to ask the only question that really mattered to me. "And your ma?"

Andy met my stare. His eyes were a mix of pain, sorrow, and anger.

"Not so good, Mount. The worse things get, the more he drinks." Andy's eyes filled. "The more he drinks, the meaner he gets." He had to look down to continue, the tears spilt out and dripped off the end of his nose. "I'm scared, Mount. Mom is scared too."

"Has he beat you or your momma?" I was instantly enraged. Red hot angry. Murderously mad.

"No…" Andy was shaking his head. "Nothing you could call a beating…yet. He's slapped me a few times…and shoved us both. Mom has bruises from him grabbing her arms. The tantrums are the worst part. You've seen how he gets, Mount. He's an inch away from your face, and screams and carries on like a wild man."

"You think he'll hurt either of you?"

"I think it's just a matter of time…if it hasn't happened already."

And suddenly Andy got kinda uncomfortable and wouldn't meet my gaze. I could tell he was pondering something; debating with himself.

My packhorse had wandered around the bend below the cottonwoods, and was grazin' beside the creek. I dismounted and spent a minute checking the packs and cinches to give Andy time to think. When I mounted up and we headed back to the cabin he'd made his decision.

"The night I left…" I had a hunch that I knew what was coming. "The night I left, father accused mother of being in love with you, Mount." Andy's eyes started to leak again and his lower lip trembled. "He screamed at her that the two of you had been lovers the whole trip. That mom loved you more than him."

"Andy, I…"

"It's true, Mount!"

"The hell it is!" I reined up way harder than I needed to. "Your ma and I never…"

"The love, Mount!" He had to really yell to interrupt my screamin'.

"Huh?"

"I said the love…the part about her loving you. It's true. I know you and she didn't…you know, but Mount, mother has been in love with you since about halfway through the trip to Oregon City." Andy's tears had dried up and he wore a shy smile. "She told me so that night, but I already knew." He turned and gazed up into the mountains. "Know what, Mount?" I could tell he was still smiling. "When we were coming cross-country…sometimes I pretended that you were my dad and father was the guide."

"Andy…"

"And during these last two years…sometimes I've pretended it was just mom and me, and we were waiting for you to come back from a trip."

"Andy…"

"I hate him, Mount!" His smile turned into a snarl. "I hate him! And mom hates him too!"

"Andy…" He didn't interrupt me that time, I just didn't know what the hell to say. "Did Sandra really say she loved me?"

"Yes, Mount. She did."

*

We rode up to the cabin. Buck was standin' in the doorway leaning against the frame.

"Thought you two hombres had rode off without me."

"Worried you did we?" I asked, as Andy and I dismounted.

68

"Hell no." Buck nodded back over his shoulder. "I got me a right fine cabin to winter in. You boys go on ahead to Oregon City."

I'd hitched the horses and walked to the cabin door. Buck and I clasped wrists and slapped shoulders.

"Good to see you, old friend."

"And you, young friend."

"Thank you for watching over Andy."

Buck laughed as he looked at Andy with admiration. "That's quite a young man there. I found him wanderin' around in circles, which ain't an easy thing to do in the mountains. He needed help, but was ready to fight when I tried to lend a hand." He shook his head at the memory. Andy stared at his boots, obviously embarrassed. "He was gonna stick me with this piddly little thing he called a knife. Yeah, that one."

Andy had reached into his pocket and held up a small folding pocket knife, his eyes stayed glued to the floor. It was a knife I'd given him nearly three years ago. It was good for cleanin' your fingernails, maybe guttin' a fish, but that was about it. We shared a laugh.

"You're welcome to stay, Buck." I put my hand on his shoulder. "But, yeah, I figure Andy and I'll be headin' out first thing in the morning."

"Sounds like there's a feller out there in Oregon City that needs to get himself an ass whoopin'." The three of us stepped into the cabin. "I'll come along if you think you'll be needin' me."

"I ain't gonna need any help at all takin' care of Mr. Andrew Worthington the Second."

"What about the rest of the folks? You may need somebody lookin' out for your backside."

"No, I don't think so." Andy answered. "Father doesn't have any friends there. Mr. Raulson the owner of the saloon lets him do odd jobs for room and board, and alcohol; but he doesn't have any friends."

"Where do you and your ma stay?"

"The three of us live in a little shack that Mr. Raulson owns, back in the alley behind the dry goods store. Ma helps Mrs. Raulson around the place too. Father sleeps somewhere else most nights."

I turned back to my old friend. I didn't need to hear any more about how Sandra was livin'. "It's up to you, Buck. I don't think I'll be needin' your help, but you're more than welcome to ride along. Or, you can stay here at the cabin and live the easy life this winter."

"Or I could head down south into the foothills for the winter like I've done for most of the last forty years." I think Buck had made up his mind before Andy and I even got back with the packhorse; unless, of course, I asked for his help.

"I've been to Oregon City. Didn't like it much," he looked around inside my cabin, "and I like your cabin right fine, Mount, but I ain't never had four walls and a roof longer than a few days. A full winter here might soften me up. I can't afford to soften up at my age."

"Well, you're welcome to stay as long as you'd like." I suddenly felt an urgency to go, like I was late for something important; which I reckon I was. "I'm gonna get our supplies and gear together."

I went outside and unpacked my packhorse, unsaddled Goldfire, and put them both in the corral. I gave 'em both a good rubdown while they were still warm.

I carried everything inside and started to go through it and repack for a longer and much more important trip.

I just hoped and prayed that I wasn't gonna be too late.

Chapter Eight

And that'd be how I found myself mounted up and headed out on a crisp autumn morning before the sun was even a promise of pink in the eastern sky. Headin' to Oregon City and the beautiful woman that I could finally admit I was in love with. Shoot, I figure I'd probably been in love with that high society lady ever since I first laid eyes on her in St. Louis when she and Andy rode up to me on their wagon along that dirt street.

My love for both Ma and son grew as our cross-country journey progressed. With every test and each life threatening challenge that confronted us, Sandra and Andy proved that they were made of tougher stuff than I'd figured. Again and again they rose up and met each ordeal head-on, and did what needed doin' to survive. I've even gotta admit that Mr. Worthington came thru once or twice along the way.

When Andy and I were mounted and ready to ride Buck stepped up beside Goldfire.

"I know I don't have to tell ya, Mount, but I'm a gonna." He almost whispered, like it was a damned secret or something. "Winter's comin'. And you know she can strike faster than a damned rattler and get meaner than a momma bear." Buck pointed up, in case I'd forgot where the sky was. "Watch the sky. Read the signs like your pa taught ya. If your goin' wasn't so danged important, I'd advise against it this time of year."

"Thanks, Buck." I reached down to give my friend a handshake. "With luck we should have a little time yet. My plan is to get through the mountains before the heavy snows fly, but you're damn sure right, if our luck runs sour we could be in three feet of snow, and deep trouble, by tonight." I nodded to the large bedrolls we each carried. "We've both got buffalo robes and coonskin hats. We each got a fire-steel and we're carryin' four big water skins. We should be just fine."

*

Andy and I made real good time in the beginning.

There was no headin' west from the cabin, not with the mountains there. They were a steep and rugged wall that climbed up to over ten-thousand feet. Instead, we followed Sweetgrass Creek downstream until it emptied into the Yellowstone.

Then we followed the Yellowstone River upstream for two days until it turned and disappeared up into the valley. We'd stayed on the north side of the river because I knew it'd be turning south where it ran down from the high country. We traveled through mostly rolling hills covered with dead yellow grass, sagebrush, juniper bushes, and cactus.

The smaller rivers and streams that fed the Yellowstone were mostly nothin' but dried up channels, being late in the year like it was. Some of the shady spots, higher up in the foothills, had a light coverin' of snow already.

Watching that river meander down from that valley got me thinkin' about how only a little more than a week had passed since I'd buried my good friend, Patch, beside Yellowstone Lake, the source of that mighty river; somewhere over that distant mountain ridge that made up the horizon. Rememberin' Patch, and some of the times we'd had, put me in a melancholy frame of mind.

This ole mountain man ain't often glad to leave behind a beautiful mountain valley, and the one that the Yellowstone snakes its way down through is as near to paradise as this ole boy has ever seen, but there were just too many bad memories up that valley. I was happy to move on.

*

When I'd come home from Oregon City, two years previous, I followed the Columbia River upstream for a couple days then headed northeast. I traveled across the plains for several days and then spent most of the rest of the trip working my way through rough and rugged mountains.

I had planned a different route for Andy and me. It was a little round-a-bout, but should be faster, with a lot less hard country to pass through. Although we still had plenty of peaks and valleys to negotiate before gettin' to our destination.

The first mountain range came the day after leaving the Yellowstone River. There was a mighty impressive horizon to our south made up of seven and eight thousand foot snow covered peaks; the two tallest bein' Canyon Peak and Pine Peak. To the north was a plateau that flattened out at around six thousand feet.

The ridge connecting north and south circled around in front of us. There was a natural pass through a fairly low saddle just to the southwest. There hadn't been a whole lot of snow yet, and we were able to get through without so much as a hint of trouble.

Two days out from crossin' that ridge another mountain range grew up in front of us. We dropped down to the south, passin' to the east of Hollowtop Mountain, and then worked our way west through the pass between Hollowtop and ole' Baldy Peak.

The travelin' was slow and hard. The days were cool and the nights got bone-freezin' cold. We'd hunker down beside the fire inside our buffalo robes and fur hats, catching short cat-naps between stoking the fire.

Several times we were forced to backtrack when we came up against an impassible box canyon or a thousand foot drop to the valley floor.

After finally makin' our way back down to the low country we traversed it to the southwest, meandering along following the easiest trail, as long as it was going generally in the proper direction.

Even hurryin' like we were, and constantly fighting a mighty strong sense of urgency, we still couldn't help but appreciate the beauty of the land. As we traveled through the low country, the stumpy little foothills to the north and the plains to the south were mostly covered with dead grass and sagebrush. As the hills got closer to the mountains they grew taller and wore a thick coat of pine forest. Behind the foothills another range of the vast Rocky Mountains continued to grow until their jagged, majestic summits were lost in the clouds.

We spent the next two and a half days travelin' south through sagebrush covered hills cut up by small rivers and large streams. Some still had water, but most didn't. The water courses were lined with different types of trees and lots of willow patches. We traveled upstream following a couple of different rivers. The weather held; it was chilly, but uneventful.

The mountains closed in from both the left and right, and early afternoon of that third day we headed up into the mountains again makin' for the lowest spot I saw.

And, well now, that's when our luck went straight to hell.

That ole bitch, Mother Nature, musta had somethin' damned special she was celebrating because she threw one hell of a party.

The blizzard hit us at a place I named Indian Head Rock. We were about halfway up the north face of the mountain, headed for the pass. The profile of the mountainside had been shaped by nature to look like a wise ole Indian chief.

We traversed in front of the slightly open mouth of the Indian head that Mother Nature had carved into the mountain using the wind, snow, and driving rain. High above us the tall forehead and deep-set eye sockets led down to the distinctive hawk-like nose. Below the Indian's mouth, the prominent chin sorta melted into the side of the mountain in a jumble of rocks and dirt, and became a dangerous shale-rock slide area. We crossed above the shale field, just below the Indian's lower lip.

As we gained altitude it'd gotten colder, but not unbearably so. Andy and I were both able to hunker down inside our buffalo robes with our coonskin hats pulled down tight and stayed comfortable enough.

As my old friend Buck had warned, high mountain storms tend to be sneaky; creepin' up on you and striking fast as a snake. The storm that hit us moved in even faster than that.

I first noticed a few lazy snowflakes drifting on just a whisper of a breeze. The sky had been nearly white and real high all day long. Quicker than the flick of a whitetail's flag the sky turned a shade darker and dropped right down on top of us. A breath later it was snowin' like the good Lord planned on coverin' the earth in white.

I was looking for a place where we could hole up and sit out the storm when the wind hit.

All of a sudden the snow that'd been falling so thick it was hard to take a breath, was blowin' sideways and movin' fast enough to sting. Andy and I stopped to tie bandanas around our faces and pieces of deerskin around our hands so we didn't have as much skin showing. The couple of small patches of bare skin that were exposed got whipped and battered.

"Move into the mountain!" I yelled into the wind. I waved with both arms before changing directions, hoping that Andy would see me. He and Skyhawk were only a few feet behind my packhorse, but they were nothing but ghostly images struggling through the raging storm.

As I guided Goldfire and the packhorse closer in under the protective face of the cliff that towered above us, I squinted back over my shoulder through the blowing snow to make sure that Andy followed.

We hadn't gone far before we found shelter, which was a damn good thing 'cause I ain't sure how far we could've made it in a storm like that.

We rounded a sharp bend in the near vertical mountainside. The move put the wind to our backs so we were able to take a breath and could see several feet in front of us. There to our right was a large crevice in the mountainside. What forces of nature could split granite like that, I can't imagine; but Andy and I were mighty happy to see it.

Even sunk down inside our buffalo robes and coonskin hats, the wind was able to get to us. Andy and I were startin' to freeze.

We needed better protection. The wind howling from behind us made talkin' possible as long as we screamed real loud.

"Do your best to clear out that snow." I shouted, motioning to the back of the fissure. We were out of the direct blast from the wind, but it swirled and twisted around us like a damned tornado, and howled past the opening like a crazed banshee.

We dismounted and as Andy labored through the already knee-deep snow, I unsheathed my knife, lowered my head into the wind, and bulled my way back to some large pine trees that grew on the downhill side of the trail.

By the time I got back with all the pine boughs I could carry, Andy had done a fine job of clearing the ground-snow from what was going to be our shelter. Using two of the large limbs, we swept the ground clear the best we could and then began building our shelter.

We laid down a groundcover of branches and then began building the wall by weaving the boughs together. It took another hurried trip for more pine boughs, but we ended up with a fairly snug little lean-to. There was room for both of us and our bedrolls. We could even move around and stretch a little, although neither of us could stand up.

There was just enough room at the opening of the gap for the horses to be somewhat protected. We left them loaded, except for our bedrolls, some food, and two of our water skins. We didn't bother tethering the horses. I knew they wouldn't be going far. I could only pray that the storm wouldn't last too long.

Once we sealed shut our little hideaway, I heard the horses moving and talking to each other, as they crowded further into our opening in the mountainside. The woven mesh of boughs that protected us moved and settled a little as the horses crowded against it, not only protecting themselves the best they could, but also making our shelter just that much warmer and more protected.

Chapter Nine

And then time slowed to a crawl, no faster than a snail with a bad case of lazy.

For awhile we heard and felt the horses shifting around and snickering back and forth; but soon those noises faded away and we were left in a world where the only sound was the muffled howling of the wind.

As the blizzard continued to rage on, the blowing and swirling snow piled up over our shelter. The dim light that we'd started with faded; only partly due to the fact that evening was comin' on. It didn't take long and our world was as dark as it was silent. Even the distant sound of the wind had become hushed.

With the utter darkness and the near silence, I worried some about our little sanctuary becoming airtight and the two of us suffocating, but we never ran out of crisp, cold mountain air.

It's damn near impossible to judge time when you got nothing to judge it by. In total darkness with only the faint, distant sound of wind, it's easy to convince yourself that the world has plumb ground to a stop; and everyone and everything is trapped in that same frozen moment.

Andy and I sat in silence for a long time. It was cold, but wrapped in our robes and coonskin hats we weren't in any danger of freezin' to death. We both squirmed around some to stay warm and to ward off stiffness; but neither of us seemed to have much to say; both lost in our own daydreams.

Then, after what seemed like hours with the two of us havin' nothing to say, slowly we began to talkin', and once we commenced to jabberin' we couldn't stop.

We reminisced about the seven month long journey we'd made across the country. It was hard to believe that it'd been nearly three years since that previous adventure had begun. We remembered the good times and the bad. I could still hear the terror in Andy's voice as we talked about when he'd been captured by the Indians. We laughed as we relived his daring escape.

I told him a few of my mountain man adventure stories; each the gospel truth of course.

I told him about the time that I'd ridden a stampeding buffalo off sacrifice cliff and the both of us were kilt at the bottom.

I told about the time me and ole Eagle Ellis was ambushed by Indians and stuck with so damn many arrows we couldn't count 'em all. We both died out there on that prairie.

Then there was that time I was nearly out of my mind with the fever and wandered smack dab into a rattlesnake den. I died several horrible deaths that day, but the fever killed every damn snake in the den.

I didn't think about it before I started that particular story, but it may not have been the best choice of tales to tell. Even in the dark I could sense Andy tense up as he remembered his own experience with a rattlesnake den, and how close he'd come to his own death.

And we talked about Sandra.

"Like I said, Mount, she loves you."

Andy's ma had confided in him that she'd fallen in love with me during our cross country adventure despite trying to deny those feelings.

How a woman that beautiful and sophisticated could fall in love with a big ole ugly mountain man like me, I surely don't understand; but I ain't gonna argue the fact.

I think Sandra and Andy were *both* more aware than I was about how I'd fallen head over heels in love with her. Like Sandra, I too had tried my damndest not to heed those feelings; feelings that I couldn't do anything about.

Mr. Worthington had been an arrogant, demanding tyrant the entire trip, but he'd also been Sandra's husband. I was raised up to believe that an honorable man doesn't court feelings for a married woman; so I'd done my best to deny those feelings.

As we continued to wait out the storm, Andy told me again how things had started to go bad for Mr. Worthington, and how he'd begun to take his frustrations out on his wife and son. The worse things got the more he drank. The more he drank the meaner he got. The meaner he got the worse things were for Sandra and Andy.

By the time Andy left to come find me, the shouting, screaming, and accusing was threatening to turn into physical violence. The thought of that man screaming at and shoving around the woman I loved made me see red. The thought of that bastard physically hurting Sandra in any way nearly drove me mad.

I sure was itchin' to get through to Oregon City and help the woman I loved. I felt as helpless as a beetle in the path of a stampede as I sat in that damn crack in the mountain.

*

Now, some of you folks might be wonderin'; when you're sitting in a fissure in a mountainside all covered with pine boughs and a few feet of snow, how do you know when the storm dies down and it's time to come out?

Damned if I know.

I slowly became aware of the fact that we couldn't hear the wind howling anymore and I was debating whether it'd be safe to come out when the issue was decided for us.

I ain't sure what moved or shifted, but we felt something happen above us. Just a touch of powdery snow drifted down through the pine boughs, then suddenly all those branches and the several feet of snow that'd been piled on top came crashing down on our heads.

And it happened fast as lightning.

I had time to *think* about layin' over Andy to protect him, but didn't have time to get there. I didn't get more than leaned forward when the limbs and snow drove me to the ground.

My six and a half feet was squashed into about a three foot square; and let me tell ya folks, that ain't an easy task. And it's painful as hell.

I shoved back against the branches that held me down and gouged into my neck, and they moved some. Andy and I were both danged lucky that we was wearin' those buffalo robes and coonskin hats, or we could've been hurt a lot worse. I forced myself up and around till I was on my hands and knees and could muster some leverage.

"Andy?" I tried to feel for him, but felt nothing but snow and branches. "Andy!"

"Mount."

It sounded like he was callin' from a mile away, but even at that I could hear the fear and pain in his voice.

"I'm comin' Andy!" I couldn't've been more concerned with Andy's wellbeing if the boy had been my own flesh and blood.

I arched my back to make more room, worked my feet underneath me, and then spreading my arms wide I exploded upward.

And scared the hell outta the horses!

I came busting up outta that pile of limbs and snow with all the force my legs and back could muster. I sent branches and snow flyin' thirty feet in every direction. All three horses neighed loudly and reared back onto their hind legs; granted the packhorse didn't get her front feet too far off the ground. All three had their ears pinned back, eyes wide, and nostrils flaring.

It was gettin' light over the ridge to the east and appeared to be shortly before sunrise; although nobody would be seein' the sun that day. We'd been in our manmade cave all night.

I wondered later if maybe Goldfire hadn't been the cause of the cave-in to let us know it was time to get moving.

Off to my right was a snow covered mound that had to be Andy. I scrambled over and reached for it. There was a determined grunt from under the mound, and then Andy shot out of the collapsed shelter sending up his own shower of snow and branches. And the top of his head clobbered me square in the nose. Andy's coonskin hat didn't do much to soften the blow.

The force of the hit knocked me back onto my butt, blood already turning my mustache and beard crimson, and once again I saw those pretty, sparkly lights.

For the next few minutes we sat there. I sat on the ground bleedin' into the snow. Andy squatted a few feet away doin' a good job of looking concerned and guilty while he tried hard not to laugh.

The blood finally slowed to a stop, and after I'd blown everything clear I could breathe as good as always so I didn't figure nothin' was broke.

"You okay, Mount? I really am sorry."

"Yeah, I think so. It weren't your fault." I gave him a good hard slap on the back and we turned to survey our predicament.

The blizzard had blown itself out, but the snow hadn't quite stopped. The sky was still real close, and had lightened up again so it was only a shade darker than the fresh snow that covered the ground. I was glad the sun wasn't shinning; it would've blinded us.

Now, the both of us were as tired as two fellers can get, and my face hurt like hell, but I decided we needed to get over that damn mountain ridge while we still had a chance to make it. So despite bein' bone tired, we packed our gear, mounted up and continued on our way.

The remainder of the trip up and over the top and halfway down the other side, Goldfire had to bust a trail through the snow. Sometimes it was knee high, sometimes chest deep. And once again that magnificent stallion awed me with his strength and stamina.

By the time we made camp that night we'd made it most of the way down the far side.

By midmorning of the following day we were back down into the low country. And we'd stay on the prairie for a week or more while we skirted around under the mountains. If I'd figured right we'd meet up with the Oregon Trail, and the route we'd taken three years earlier, around Fort Boise.

It'd be about five days before Andy and I'd be fighting for our lives again.

*

There hadn't been a speck of Indian trouble in them parts for a long spell. The Makah and Nez Perce tribes laid claim to most of the land west of the Rockies and north of the Columbia River, and they'd made peace with the few settlers that had moved into the area.

Now, that didn't mean that I wasn't worried about possible Indian problems. I'd learned my lesson while leadin' Andy's family, when I'd allowed a war party to capture all four of us. I was always on guard.

From the time Andy and I started our journey I'd been mindful of the possibility. I hadn't said anything to Andy because I didn't expect any trouble, and didn't see any good in puttin' thoughts into his head and scarin' him for no reason, but I knew the chance of an Indian attack was always there.

I tried to pick our route to keep hidden as much as possible. A lot of the time there wasn't nothin' more than a damned sagebrush or juniper bush for cover. Now and again there'd be a sparse line of puny trees that marked a watercourse; most of 'em dry that time of year. We rode the trees when we could, or maybe just followed along the bottom of a dry creek bed.

As we rode I kept one eye on the horizon both left and right. At night I didn't stand guard, but I made damn sure that we were tucked away somewhere so no wandering braves would stumble across us. And I slept with one eye and both ears open.

And all my watchin' and frettin' and missin' sleep didn't amount to a pile of rat droppings.

When the attack came, it came fast as a hummingbird's wings, and fierce as a cornered cougar. And it came from above us. The one direction I wasn't lookin'.

We were riding a dry creek bed. There were a lot of large rocks, driftwood, and the like, so the movin' was slow, mostly just letting Goldfire and Skyhawk pick their way.

We came to a spot where the creek made a sharp right turn. The left bank had been undercut till it was a ten foot wall of sandstone and dried mud. There were maybe half a dozen old cottonwoods (a rare sight in them parts) that grew on either side, with their branches intertwined over the creek.

We were under those overhanging limbs when all hell broke loose.

Goldfire was the first to sense somethin' was wrong. His ears perked up, his head followed, and he bolted for safety; but when he cleared the trees I wasn't on his back anymore.

When Goldfire's head came up I had just enough time to wonder why before two Indian braves dropped from the trees and tore me from the saddle.

One of them damned redskins landed square on my head, ripping my hat off in the process. The other landed on the bedroll behind me. They both grabbed a hold and forced me off the right side. We hadn't even stopped bouncin' when at least four more savages leapt screamin' off that ten foot sandstone embankment and joined in the fracas. Two of them jumped on me.

I couldn't even put up a fight at first. When we hit the ground both those damned savages were on top of me. All the air left me in a rush and I wasn't able to do much fightin' until it came back.

Now, I don't know if any of you folks have had that distinct pleasure of havin' the wind knocked out of you, but take it from a feller who knows. You're pretty sure that you're gonna die. And no matter how hard you try to take that breath, it ain't comin' in until those lungs are ready. It only lasts a few seconds, but they're the longest seconds of your life.

By the time I could finally draw a breath those bastards had rolled me over onto my stomach. Two sat on my legs, one on my head, and one astride my back; that particular Indian was wrappin' a leather strap around my wrists.

Those twin bellows in my chest hitched and shuddered and finally kicked in. I could breathe, but I couldn't move.

And then I saw Andy.

I was lookin' through the crook in the leg of the Indian that sat on my head. While my lungs were suckin' up dirt with each gasp for air, my eyes focused on what was happening beside me.

There were three Indians holdin' Andy down, and one of them was strapping his wrists together too. I was close enough to see into Andy's eyes.

Horror. Pure, raw terror. Mind numbing, death dealing fear.

Andy had spent a couple weeks alone in an Indian camp as a captive. He still went pale and got a bad case of the shakes even talkin' about it.

And that's when I made a decision that I probably had no right to make.

That look in Andy's panic filled eyes screamed at me that he'd rather die than be captured again. So that's the decision I made.

The two of us were either getting away, or we were gonna die tryin'.

I felt that leather strap begin to tighten down on my wrists, and I knew I had to make my move. I could feel that the Indian astride my back was leanin' just a touch to the right, so that's the way I went.

I twisted with all the strength and determination that I could muster, and was rewarded with a grunt of surprise as the young brave went flyin'. At the same instant I jerked my legs up real fast, and the two sittin' on them ended up on their butts in the dirt. I was now on my back with my legs pulled tight to my chest. I kicked out with both feet and hit the closest one in the face. He was out of the fight. That left three.

The feller sittin' on my head had a grip on my shoulders and went with my roll. As I flipped over and pushed onto my hands and knees to get up he was directly in front of me, also on his hands and knees.

I gathered my feet under me and pushed off with all my might (hell, it'd worked pretty good for Andy and he hadn't even been tryin'). I lowered my head and the top of my rock-hard skull smashed into his face. I heard bones crunch and felt blood squirt as he was driven back onto his haunches then crumpled over onto his side. Another redskin was out of the fight.

As I gained my feet I risked a glance over to where the Indians had Andy pinned to the ground. Only they didn't have him pinned anymore.

Apparently he and I had come to similar conclusions concerning our future and he'd commenced to fighting back too.

I'd been busy saving my own skin, but when I risked a glance to my right, Andy was the only one standin'. The three Indian braves were sprawled on the ground; but two of them were climbing to their feet.

And that second that I spent watching them nearly cost me my life. A streaking shadow snapped my head around in time to see a razor sharp tomahawk aiming to split my head open.

I barely got an arm up to deflect it, and instead of splitting open my skull, the damn thing sliced off the top of my left ear. I screamed in pain and anger, and picked that bastard up by the neck and shook him like a wild dog killin' a jackrabbit.

And then all of a sudden I was being ridden to the ground with two Indian braves on my back. The feller I had my hands around was out of the fight; it's hard to tussle with a broken neck.

As I hit the ground I rolled hard; to the left this time. It'd worked before and it worked again. Both savages grunted when they slammed into the frozen ground. I spun around, got to my knees, and before they could crawl away, I grabbed one by the neck and one by the hair. I thumped their heads together once to get their attention, and then proceeded to slam their skulls against the ground; again and again and....

When I ran out of breath and my arms burned from lifting the weight, I stopped. I realized that my eyes were filled with tears of rage. I dropped the two unconscious men and wiped angrily at my eyes to clear them.

Still half blind I climbed to my feet and rushed to go help Andy.

And as my eyes cleared I realized that it was those Indian braves that needed the savin'.

Andy was standing between two unconscious bodies. He would kick one, then turn and kick the other, then repeat the process. He kept at it until I wrapped my arms around him and held him tight. He turned, buried his face in my buffalo robe, and commenced to crying like a baby.

As I held him I took stock of our enemies. One of them, I believe it was the first one Andy had thrown off, was a small figure off in the distance; horse and rider galloping across the prairie.

As I turned to the others, the two I'd pounded the ground with were slowly climbing to their feet. They stood unsteadily side by side, and I think even considered attacking again for a couple seconds. I figure they maybe saw somethin' in my eyes that changed their minds.

They turned and scrambled up the embankment on the far side of the creek bed. A moment later they went galloping off into the prairie chasing after their friend.

Of the five Indians that remained on the ground, the two Andy had been kickin', weren't going to be a threat ever again; neither was the one who's neck I'd snapped. The one I'd head butted was still out cold. And the one I'd booted in the face was on his stomach with his hands to his mug, rolling from side to side and moaning softly.

I figured we were safe enough. I just stood and held Andy, and felt love and concern for him as strong as any father could feel for a son.

Chapter Ten

We found our horses on the bluff above the creek. They were grazing right next to the Indian ponies. A lesson us two-legged critters could learn from.

Andy refused to take any of the Indian's possessions, so we gathered what was ours, I doctored my cut ear, and we headed out. We rode at a fast trot, side by side along the creek bank so we could make good time.

He'd been quiet and far off since we'd hit the trail. I reckoned I knew what was botherin' him, and gave him time to chew on it. After a few miles he finally spoke up.

"You think those two Indians are dead, Mount?"

"Well, I don't rightly know, Andy." I lied. He wasn't lookin' at me, but staring down at his hands. "There was four of 'em that hadn't moved by the time we left; but that don't necessarily mean nothin'."

"I've never killed anyone," he said; like there was any chance that he had. "Heck, I've never even beat anybody up before. I don't think I like the feeling."

"Good."

Andy looked up in surprise at my answer.

"But...shouldn't I be happy or feel a little proud maybe...something like that?" He asked "'Cause I don't feel nothing but lousy."

"Andy, it's a rugged, dangerous country out here, and well, sometimes you just gotta fight so you can go on breathin'. You gotta kill or you're gonna get kilt."

He continued to look at me with a troubled expression.

"And today was one of those times. We did what needed done for us to survive, but that don't mean you should enjoy it. Killin' a man under any circumstances is a hard thing. And if it's ever anything else, well, then *that's* when you need to start worryin'."

Andy understood what I was sayin', and he knew I was right, but it still took a few days before he came to some sort of understanding with his own self, and was able to move on.

And we were able to move on for exactly three more days before we found ourselves in our next life or death struggle.

*

Tree covered foothills and pretty, rolling meadows were off in the distance to our north. The territory we traveled through had mostly one feature; flat. For miles in any direction the most remarkable sight was sagebrush and juniper bushes.

So far we'd outrun the snow, but it was still gettin' colder; considerably colder during the day and cold enough to kill a man at night.

Sagebrush burns hot; hot and fast. Too damn fast. There was no lack of brush for a fire, but you needed to constantly feed it. There was no throwin' a big ole log on the fire and lying down to sleep.

Andy and I tried a fire a couple of nights. We took turns; one stoking the fire while the other rested, but we decided it was easier and just as restful to simply pull our coonskins down over our ears, and hunker down inside those heavy buffalo robes and try to doze in the saddle.

I'd heard stories of Indian hunting parties that'd been caught unawares by an early season storm, and had survived for days in frigid temperatures just wearin' a loincloth and covered head to toe in a buffalo robe.

The horses didn't seem to mind stayin' on the move either; they were warmer. We allowed 'em to set their own pace and they seemed content to keep up a steady walk. There was just enough groundcover for them to stay fed, but water became a problem.

We carried four big water skins. Three of 'em were empty and the fourth was goin' fast. I was expecting to meet up with the

Snake River, or come across Fort Boise any day, but there's a hell of a difference between one day and three or four days when you're providin' water for two men and three horses.

Early one afternoon we happened across a small sinkhole in the sandy soil. At the bottom of the hole was a pool of water. Andy was the one who spotted it.

"Look, Mount!" He pointed and reined Skyhawk to the right. "Water!"

Before I got there he was off his horse and approaching the pool.

"Whoa, boy." I called out. "Hang on there."

"What, Mount?"

"That's still water." I dismounted and joined Andy beside the hole.

"Huh?"

"I mean it ain't moving. Mighty bad things can live in stagnant water. If it ain't movin' you need to check it out real careful."

"That makes sense."

"Damn right it does, boy. Pay attention and learn."

I dropped to my knees and put my face down close to the water. There was a few tiny "somethins" floating around, but mostly it looked clear. I inhaled deeply; it smelled like a cold, sweet mountain spring. I dipped my hand and tasted it, and it tasted as good as any water I'd ever had. I stood up and gave Andy the go ahead.

"Seems okay to me. Drink your fill, and then we'll water the horses." I went to get one of the water skins. The pool wasn't very deep, but I figured I could slop one skin partially full.

Andy had just finished drinkin' when I got back.

"Yes sir that tastes awfully good." He wiped a drop off his bearded chin. "A lot better than that old, stale water we've been drinking."

"I'll try to get some in this skin. Once we get to the Snake or Columbia water won't be a problem clear to Oregon City."

"How long you figure that to be, Mount? Oregon City I mean."

Something in his voice made me look up. The worry and concern was smeared all over his face and spilling from his eyes. Andy had turned from a young man to a little boy who missed his mama.

"Well now, I ain't rightly sure, Andy." I tried my best to figure it. "If nothin' happens to slow us down, I'm hoping we meet up with the Columbia River within the next couple of days. Then figure four, maybe five days along the Columbia, then a day south along the Willamette River to Oregon City."

Andy turned back and got another couple swallows of water. I drank another mouthful and slopped a little into the skin, and then we let the horses drink their fill.

And within the hour we were all, including the horses, sicker than rabid dogs. Andy was the worst of all. I don't know what poison it was in that water, but it very nearly killed the boy I'd begun to think of as my son.

I hadn't drunk nearly as much as Andy, and the horses were big and strong enough not to be in danger of dying, but Andy was in real trouble.

He lay on his side with his arms clutching his knees to his chest, and there was horrible stuff comin' out both ends of that young man that I won't even try to describe.

You're welcome.

I had my own problems going on. My guts cramped up and it felt like a couple of bull elk were lockin' horns in there. I don't know what I would've done for Andy, but I felt guilty that for quite a spell I couldn't even offer help.

All three horses stood fifty feet away with their heads hung low and fertilized the ground. By the time the worst had passed for me, the horses were back to grazing.

Andy had slipped into the deliriums. He still had his arms around his knees and he rocked back and forth in his own filth; moaning, mumbling, and crying. His whole body shook from the cold as sweat poured off him. I knelt beside him with my hand on his shoulder, whispered encouragement, and felt helpless as a leaf caught in floodwater.

"Lord..." Must've been some dust or somethin' had gotten into my eyes. I wiped 'em dry and gazed up to heaven. "Lord, I know that we ain't talked much lately. Hell...uh, I mean, heck, I think the last time may've been when Patch was kilt, but, uh, Lord, this boy laying here is sufferin' something awful, and well, he's become mighty important to me, and uh, well, please Lord, Sir, could you help ease his pain, and please don't let him...uh, Sir, please don't let...uh, Lord, I reckon you know what I'm tryin' to get at. Please and thank you, Sir. Amen."

It was late in the evening when Andy's cramping started to let up and his mind began to unmuddle. He was finally able to unfold himself and stretch out that long, lanky body of his.

I started forcing good water into him from our last, nearly empty, skin. It may've been a bit stale, but it was healthy water, and Andy couldn't've had a good spit worth of fluid left in him.

He was weak as a newborn baby. It was a perfectly clear night which meant it got teeth chatterin' cold, but I couldn't leave Andy; he was conscious but still dazed, like he was off somewhere else.

The clear night also meant the sky was plumb overflowing with stars. So, for a long time we sat huddled together inside our robes, each in our own world, starin' up at the sparkling heavens. I made sure Andy took a sip of water every minute or so.

By the time the cold had wormed its way inside our robes, Andy had recovered enough that I could leave him alone for a spell. We needed a fire.

We both cleaned up the best we could and then I had Andy bundle up inside his robe and lay down. Until I got the fire blazin' that buffalo robe shook like a small weed in a big wind.

All the rest of the night I fetched sagebrush to keep that fire goin'. I found a few pieces of dead juniper close by too; it burnt a little bit longer. Andy got his first good night sleep in a long time.

Next morning we both felt like we'd been kicked in the stomach by a bull and Andy was still weak as a baby kitten, but we were able to travel.

Andy felt a little better the next day, and better yet the next. That second day I shot three big jackrabbits and we had our first hot meal in quite a spell.

*

So, I ain't sure how I managed it, but somehow we plumb missed Fort Boise. I figure we must've dropped down south of the fort.

And we crossed the Oregon Trail someplace without even noticing it too. That didn't surprise me none. The ground was pretty hard and covered in short grass and the Oregon Trail was fairly new and little used. It completely disappeared plenty of times during its cross-country run. We probably passed right over the trail and didn't even notice it.

Two days after our jackrabbit supper we got to the Snake River.

It was a cold, cloudy afternoon, made even colder by a light, but steady, breeze. We gathered enough dry wood and brush for a large fire, and then we both stripped down and took a much needed bath. That river water was ice cold. The fire afterwards felt like home.

It'd been nearly three years since I guided the Worthington family along that very river on our way to Oregon City. It brought back a lot of memories of that previous trip. Most of 'em bad.

On that previous trip we'd followed the Snake through the mountains and beyond. That meant we had to traverse Hell's Canyon. We very nearly didn't make it out the other side that first time. I didn't reckon I wanted to try our luck through that blasted country again.

And besides, beyond the canyon, that river makes a big loop up to the northwest and then back southwest before emptying into The Columbia River. I didn't figure on doing that loop again either, so rather than follow the river downstream we crossed it and headed west.

We had to meander down to the south a piece to stay out of the high country. Two days past the Snake River we spent a night on the shore of Malheur Lake.

Then it was back to the northwest. My plan was pretty much to stay to the lowest route I could find. We weaved and wound our way through some mighty varied country for another four more days before finally meetin' up with the Columbia River.

We traveled through grass covered prairie where all we saw was sagebrush, juniper bushes, and a lone scrub pine every once in a while. The only things movin' were tumbleweeds and, now and then, some antelope.

Then we came across sand dunes that stretched away as far as the eye could see. There was nothin' movin' there at all. We were able to skirt the dunes around to the east.

Then it was back to the grassy prairie for a while. And the whole time we had the mountains to the northeast and to our west. Sometimes close enough to smell the pine, sometimes just a saw-tooth line on the horizon.

When we finally met up with the Columbia, I figured we must've been close to a hundred miles west of where we'd joined up with that mighty river before.

A snow covered Mount Hood stood off in the distance to the southwest.

Downstream about twenty miles we came across a Methodist Mission named The Wascopam, after the native Wasco Indians. A Mr. and Mrs. Bartholomew Calloway ran the place. They were fine folks and very hospitable to Andy and I, and Edna Calloway was a mighty good cook.

The last hot bath I'd had was at Fort Granger durin' Rendezvous; unless you counted my soakin' in the hot pots. It felt mighty good to get a few layers of grime off and then sink back in that tub of hot water and relax.

They even offered us a strap and a straight-edge, but when Andy decided to keep his beard, I decided I'd keep mine too.

*

Crossing over to the north side of the river hadn't been possible when traveling with the Worthingtons. It'd been about two months earlier in the year and the Columbia had been running too much water to cross. I recalled the hard time we'd had traveling the rugged south bank; several times having to back off the river for miles before we could find a route.

When Andy and I got there that November, the Columbia was running low enough that fording the river was a choice; as long as we made the crossing before the series of rapids and waterfalls. I decided we'd do it.

Goldfire and Skyhawk both were experienced river swimmers by then. The strong current and ice cold water didn't hardly slow 'em down at all. The packhorse didn't like crossin' none, but didn't have any choice in the matter.

Traveling the north bank of the Columbia was considerably easier than being on the southern side; at least for the first day and a half. We followed a dry creek bed up onto a flat plateau that bordered the river. We were probably a thousand feet above the river and the land was mostly barren so the travelin' was easy as loungin' on a summer day.

The southern side of the river was mostly barren at that point too, but it was much more cut up by runoffs and drainages, with vertical cliffs dropping right down into the water in some places.

By midmorning of the second day things had begun to even out considerably. The land got rough along both banks of the river. And in the distance we watched the Cascade Mountains grow outta the horizon. The riding got harder as the lookin' got a whole lot easier.

As the mountains drew closer, the trees and a variety of groundcovers returned to the hills. By late afternoon we were pickin' our way through pine covered foothills. Sometimes the river ran right beside us, sometimes we couldn't even hear it's roar as we made our way around a particularly deep ravine. Each time we reached a high spot where we could look off into the distance the mountains were a touch closer.

Even though it was November and low water, there was another waterfall every couple miles as the river negotiated a series of steps and shelves.

All the leaf bearing trees were in their full autumn finery. The gold, orange, and red leaves combined with all the different shades of brown and green from the ground foliage and thick blankets of moss that covered most everything made for awful pretty country. A bright blue sky with snow-white clouds and a blazing yellow sun looked down on it all.

The only real trouble we had along the Columbia was crossin' one of the bigger tributaries. I think it may've been the Wind River.

I'd untied the packhorse from my saddle and wrapped the rope around my wrist. I'd done it before; my thinking bein' that if the packhorse went down I could drop the rope. After all, it ain't like I was gonna pull her up if she fell.

And damned if that ain't exactly what she did. The flaw in my plan was the fact that when it happened I wasn't payin' a lick of attention to the packhorse. Goldfire was chest deep in a surprisingly strong current, and I was standing high in my stirrups tryin' to stay as dry as I could, and watching the water ahead for danger.

Quicker than a bee sting, the lead rope that I had loosely wrapped around my wrist tightened up like the noose around a horse thief's neck and jerked me off backwards into the freezing water.

Now, I've explained before how I don't swim much better than a fish can fly. Wearin' calf-high moccasins and heavy deerskins, all wrapped up inside thirty pounds of buffalo robe, I sunk like a waterlogged rock.

The current was strong, the water was damn cold, and the river channel was filled with boulders and deadfall. As I tumbled and bounced down the river I could hear the roar of a waterfall somewhere downriver; and not very damn far downriver!

I finally managed to get my legs under me and kicked off the river bottom with all my might. The river was only about six feet deep, and with panic spurin' me on, I kicked hard enough to send me, moccasins, buffalo robe and all, flyin' right to the edge of the bank. I crawled onto dry land and had to lay there for a spell to gather my wits. By the time I was able to take a decent breath, I was shivering like a rattler's button.

I sat up and watched as Andy and Skyhawk made their way up the nearside bank with no problems.

Goldfire and that damned trouble makin' packhorse were both downstream grazing as they waited for the rest of us.

"Are you okay, Mount?" Andy was out of the saddle before Skyhawk had stopped; a mighty worried look on his face as he knelt down beside me.

"Bbbbuild a fffire."

I spent most of the rest of that day sittin' naked as a newborn, beside a roaring fire with my clothes and robe hung up to dry.

*

Two days later. Two days of fightin', strugglin', slippin', and slidin' to make our way into, out of, or around mountain ridges and through deep cut valleys, we came to LaCamas; named for the camas plant, the root of which is used by the Indians for food.

LaCamas along the Columbia wasn't nothin' more than a middlin' sized log cabin, a ferry for crossing the river, and two Frenchmen to operate it. As we'd made our way downstream the river had grown from all the tributaries till it would've been a mighty dangerous proposition to swim it, even late in the year like it was. And after damn near drowning in the Snake, I wasn't real anxious to ride into the Columbia.

The Frenchies were the Barteau brothers. I didn't bother to learn their first names because they was the spittin' image of each other so you couldn't tell one from the other anyway.

The ugly brother told us it'd be five dollars to get ferried across the river.

When I told them that was damned robbery, and we had fewer than three dollars cash money between the two of us, the other ugly brother laughed and inquired as to what possessions we might have worthy of trading.

The Barteau brothers ferried us across the Columbia for just under three dollars cash, a good cookin' pot, and about half a pound of jerky. It was still more than the job was worth, but I guess we didn't have much choice. I figured we'd be in Oregon City by the next night.

And we were.

Chapter Eleven

From the ferry crossing we took the Barteau brother's suggestion to cut cross-country, headed southwest rather than follow the Columbia River to its meetin' up with the Willamette and then turn south.

Just before sunset we ran into the Willamette River as it meandered northward headin' for the Columbia.

We set up our last camp and built our last fire. I didn't figure neither of us would sleep a wink, and I was surprised as hell when we both slept clear into the mornin'.

We were up and ridin' quick like, and pulled into Oregon City a little past midday. I was nervous as a fly caught in a spider web, with a big ole black widow bearin' down.

All morning long, clouds the color of trouble had been rolling in over the mountains and crowdin' the blue outta the sky. As we passed the sawmill, which was quiet except for the roar of the water, and rode into Oregon City, a light rain began to fall.

The last time I'd ridden into that town, nearly three years before, it'd been rainin' too.

The town hadn't actually changed so much as it seemed to have aged. It seemed like maybe twenty years had passed in the three years I'd been away. The place seemed to have shrunk somehow. What had been a busy, bustling town was now a quiet, sleepy memory of what it used to be.

There was no doubt that Oregon City would someday grow and thrive, but for the time being it appeared to be dryin' up and wasting away.

No one at all seemed to take notice as Andy led us down the long, muddy main street. No one took notice because there wasn't anybody around.

Businesses lined both sides of the street. Some were open, some boarded up; and they all looked old and rundown. None of the open establishments seemed to be doing much of a business.

The boardwalk that ran in front of the businesses was in bad need of repair, with split and warped boards just waitin' to trip somebody up. The river made its way over another series of steps and falls not far behind the buildings on the west side of the street.

Andy led us past the General Store and a boarded up assessor's office. We rode by a saloon and a mission house. On the east side of the street there was a large building with Worthington's painted in white on the front. The doors and windows were boarded up. Andy didn't so much as glance at it as we passed.

Behind the Dry Goods store Andy stopped beside a small cabin. Hell, it wasn't nothin' more than a simple frame shack with what looked like old reused planks slapped up for walls. If you looked at it straight on, the whole damn thing leaned a smidgen to the right.

As we dismounted Andy looked across Skyhawk's back at me. His eyes reflected the conflict ragin' in his head. His excitement of being back wrestlin' with his fear of what we were gonna find.

We tied the horses off and walked around to the door, which opened onto the alley. The leather-hinged door creaked as it opened, and Andy led me into the dark, cold one room shack. When he quickly closed the door to slow the precious heat from gettin' away, it was dark as night.

Heavy wool blankets hung over the two windows, and a half burned candle flickered weakly on a small table beside the door. Two straight back chairs were beside the table. To the side of those was a counter with a water basin. Next, set in the corner, was a small wood stove; six inch piping went straight up, out the roof. The fire had gone out, but there was still a little heat coming off the iron stove. A large, wingback chair sat in the shadows of the far corner, facing the wall.

Even after my eyes grew accustomed to the near dark, I thought the cabin was empty.

Then, as Andy moved across the room he slid one of the chairs out of the way. When it scraped against the wooden floor movement caught my eye. It came from the chair that was hidden in shadow over in the corner. My first impression was of an old lady shying away from a loud noise.

"Mom?" Andy whispered so quietly that standing right beside him I barely heard.

The silhouette in the chair stiffened.

"Mom, it's me. I'm home."

And that old lady, who it turned out wasn't an old lady at all, squealed like some sort of wild critter and exploded out of the chair and into Andy's arms.

Sandra Worthington was two or three inches shy of six feet. Only a couple years before, her and her son stood pretty much eye to eye. Andy towered over her like a cottonwood over a willow as they hugged inside that shack on that cold November afternoon.

She buried her face in his chest and he buried his in her raven hair, and the two of them commenced to carryin' on till I thought they was gonna topple over. They was cryin' and laughin' and both trying to talk at the same time.

I only heard bits and pieces, *"I'm sorry"* several times from Andy. Sandra repeated *"My baby, my boy..."* and *"So worried..."* and *"Don't you ever..."* a lot. Both said, *"I love you..."* over and over.

I reckon if my heart was ever gonna burst due to pure joy and happiness, that would've been the time.

Their "welcome home" dance eventually wound down. I figure they both just finally got tuckered out. After one final smooch that Sandra planted on Andy's cheek, they separated.

They were both still laughing thru their tears. Sandra wiped her eyes with her sleeve and started straightening Andy's mussed up hair. In her excitement to have her son home, she still hadn't noticed me standin' back there in the shadows.

"You…" Her eyes filled up again and spilled over onto her cheeks. She was smilin' from ear to ear while her lower lip trembled and shook. "You look good with the whiskers…older." One of her hands went up to cover her mouth, as if that'd stop the tears. The other hand tugged Andy's chin hair.

It was the same beautiful Sandra that I remembered; yet it wasn't. Her hair was still jet black and fell past her waist, but it no longer shined as though lit by an inner glow. It was dull and lifeless.

The body that had been straight, proud, and full of bounce was, even in her joy of having Andy back, slumped a bit. Her shoulders rolled forward and her back slightly bent as if carrying a heavy load.

And she was downright skinny! She'd never carried any extra weight on her five foot nine inch frame, but she'd never been skinny either. She'd always had just the right amount of curves in all the right places; but in that cabin, on that cold autumn afternoon, she'd become a skin-and-bones ghost of her old self.

As she continued to talk to Andy, her eyes broke from his and wandered to the right, over his shoulder. "…and don't you dare try another stunt like…" She suddenly realized what it was she was looking at. She froze up. I think she may've actually quit breathin' for a spell.

"Hello, Sandra." I just stood there wearin' a stupid grin. I wanted to run across the room, which would've been about three steps, and wrap her in my arms and declare my everlasting love.

Instead, I nodded towards Andy and mumbled. "Look who I found out wanderin' in the mountains."

And there was that wild animal screech again, and I was nearly knocked plumb off my feet when Sandra hit me. Once I was sure of my balance I bent so I could get my arms around her waist and pick her up off the floor. She put her face against my neck and I buried mine in her raven hair and we were off; having our own celebration, complete with the laughin' and cryin' and me stumbling around the room while Sandra's feet dangled in the air.

When we returned to our senses, the three of us were standing together in the middle of the room; hugging each other. Now folks, I truly believe that every person should be allowed to feel happiness like that at least once in their lifetime.

We each took a step backwards and for the first time I was able to really look at Sandra up close.

Yes, she was still the most beautiful woman I'd ever seen; but she'd changed. Her loss of weight made her face look shrunken; drawn in where her cheeks used to be, like she'd been sufferin' with a prolonged illness.

And her eyes were different. Even with the excitement of Andy and me showin' up outta the blue, Sandra's eyes held a sort of deep sadness. The stunning, dark mahogany color was still there, but her eyes didn't sparkle with life as they had before. They were beautiful eyes, glistening through her tears of joy, but they weren't the same eyes I'd known before.

And below her left eye...there, where her cheekbone pushed against the skin...was that? It was a couple inches across; pink around the edges, turning a darker red towards the middle. The exact center was scabbed over.

"Is that...?" As I realized what I was lookin' at, anger flooded through me... "Did he...?" ...and washed away my self control and any small amount of common sense that I may've started with.

Sandra's left hand came up to cover the bruise on her cheek, and her eyes dropped to the floor. It was all the answer I needed.

"That son of a bitch!" It was more of a roar than a yell. I think I even scared myself a little.

And then I was through the door, around the shack, and out into the street in the drizzling rain.

"WORTHINGTON!"

There were two saloons. One was two doors up on my side of the street. The other was about three doors down on the other side.

"Worthington!" I just stood in the middle of the street, in the mud and drizzling rain, and bellowed like a crazy man. "Worthington! You worthless bastard! Where are you?!"

Both saloon doors flew open at about the same time. The one across the street was the batwing style. Neither feller who cautiously peered out was Worthington.

In fact, I noticed that pretty much every open business along both sides of the street had at least one person standing in their doorway or pasted to a window tryin' to see what the ruckus was about.

The gentleman standing in the batwing doors waved his hand. Just once, up about shoulder high and then back to his side. It was the signal I'd been lookin' for.

When he saw me comin', the feller quickly disappeared back into the saloon.

I hit those swingin' doors like a charging ram. I'm surprised they didn't fly off the hinges.

The place was nearly empty. A bartender stood behind the counter. Three men, one of them the feller who I'd seen at the door, stood to my right, up against the bar. All three eyed me mighty curious like.

And Mr. Andrew Worthington the Second sat alone at a table in the far corner. His head was down so I couldn't see his face, but it was him alright. Both hands were resting on the table in front of him, clutching a glass of whiskey.

As I headed across the room I saw fast movement to my right and heard the unmistakable sound of a rifle hammer being drawn back. I looked to the bar and the bartender had one of those fancy, new long-rifles pointed at my chest. I stopped.

"I don't know who the hell you are stranger, but you'd best simmer down and consider your next move real careful like."

I looked from the barman to Worthington. He'd raised his head and was looking my direction. Because of the shadows I couldn't read his eyes. I took another step.

The bartender raised the rifle to his shoulder and aimed. "One more step, friend. One more and you're wearin' a bullet." I stopped again. "Hell, with this new rifle, I can probably get two in ya before you get across the room."

I debated whether to give it a try.

I figured two bullets would slow me down a bit, but with a little luck I could still get to Worthington. All I needed was a couple of seconds. Just long enough to get my hands around his neck and twist.

Sandra and Andy came running through the doors.

"Mount, no!" Sandra yelled.

"He's not worth it, Mount." Andy added.

They were both still wiping tears from their eyes. Neither of them even glanced in Mr. Worthington's direction.

"It's okay, Elton." Sandra held a palm out towards the bartender. He lowered the rifle just enough so that instead of my chest, it was aimed at my crotch.

Sandra turned back to me. I stood there as confused as I'd ever been. I looked from Mr. Worthington to Sandra to Andy, and back around again; and, believe me, I never forgot about the man who was still pointing that gun at my private parts.

"Look at him, Mount." Sandra finally glanced at the table in the corner. "Go ahead, look. He's nothing but a helpless drunk now."

"But he…" I pointed to her cheek.

"That was a week ago." Her hand came up to cover the bruise. "It was only once and I kicked him out afterwards." She hurried to add. "I haven't even seen him since."

Elton, the bartender, didn't look like he was plannin' to pull the trigger, so I walked into the shadows where Mr. Worthington sat. As I got closer, he leaned back in his chair so he could look up at me.

And Sandra was right.

Gone was the confident, arrogant, high and mighty bastard that had ordered us around like slaves for the months it took to cross the country; the man who thought that his money alone made him better, more superior, to everyone else.

In front of me sat the beaten and ruined remains of that man. His hair was unkempt and he wore several days' worth of beard; the Mr. Worthington I knew would've never allowed that. In fact, he'd gussied up with a shave and a haircut at every fort or settlement we came to along the trail.

His eyes were glassy, bloodshot, and heavy lidded, but I saw recognition dawn in them.

"Well I'll be damned." He pointed with a very unsteady hand. His words were slurred. "If it isn't the guide."

I almost felt sorry for him. Almost.

It was like seeing a proud, wild stallion caught, tamed and turned into a plow horse.

Then I recalled all the pain and suffering that man had caused for the woman and boy that I could finally admit my love for. The pity drained away and the anger flooded back.

I grabbed a handful of the worn, store-bought leather jacket and frayed flannel shirt that Worthington wore, and yanked him up out of his chair. He tried to get his legs under him, but couldn't quite manage it, so he just hung there. His whiskey breath stung my eyes and nose.

"You're to stay away from Sandra and Andy." His worn out leather jacket began to rip and the stink of his breath was awful, so I let him drop back into the chair. "As long as we're in town, you'll stay clear of the three of us."

A flicker of pride still burned somewhere deep inside him. His eyes blazed and his mouth found the old sneer that I'd seen all across the country.

"She's *my* wife…*my* son."

And he was right.

That had been the only reason that I'd ridden out of Oregon City in the first place; leavin' the woman and boy that I loved behind. It hadn't mattered how much I cared for Sandra and Andy, or what a rotten excuse for a man Mr. Worthington had been. Mr. Worthington *had* been husband and father and I just couldn't get in the way of that. It just wasn't right. But that was then.

All that didn't matter anymore.

I got down on one knee so I could look Worthington straight in his bleary eyes.

"You ain't never been a proper husband or father!" I was finally able to say what I'd felt and thought for so long. "Sandra and Andy are just possessions to you, not family. You think of them as things, to own and show off, rather than precious gifts that you need to love, treasure, and care for."

The fire died down in his eyes. I could still see glowing embers of hate for me, but it looked like all the fight in him had washed away with the whiskey and been blown away from all the wind from my speech. Hell, I don't know if I've ever strung that many words together all at once. And I wasn't done yet.

"And now…" My sneer matched the one he'd had. "Hell, you can't even take care of yourself." I looked over to where Sandra and Andy still stood, on the other side of the room. "And you've been mistreating Sandra and Andy, emotionally and physically."

"But…we…we're still married." He made one last feeble attempt to fight back; and I had to admit that he did make a damn good point. Now, I was pretty sure that there was some sorta legal mumbo-jumbo that could be done to correct the unfortunate situation, but I had no idea how to begin.

"Yeah, well, we'll have to see what can be done about that," was the best I could do. I leaned over him and poked a big meaty finger into his chest. "Just make damn sure you stay away from all three of us."

I joined Sandra and Andy and with one arm around each we left the saloon. As we went through those swingin' doors, Mr. Worthington was sitting up with his head back and draining the last of the whiskey in his glass.

The three of us walked back to that rundown cabin in silence. When we got inside, the first thing I did was pull down the wool blankets covering the two windows. It was still cloudy and wet outside, but it seemed sunshine bright in that little shack. Sandra and Andy watched me with a puzzled look.

"No more hidin' in the dark." I proclaimed. "Damned if it ain't time to start livin' again."

Sandra's eyes filled up with tears. She stepped up to me, wrapped her arms around my waist and laid her head on my chest. As I felt her breasts press against me, my ability to speak, or move, or even think proper, plumb abandoned me. All I was able to manage was to smother her in my arms and squeeze as tight as I dared.

After a couple glorious minutes we pulled apart just enough so that she could look up into my eyes. My next move was obvious all over her face. I pulled her up onto her toes, I bent down, and we joined for our first kiss.

Our lips met for just a couple of seconds, and then we parted. I opened my eyes and gazed into hers. I realized that I had a grin spread across my face wide as a prairie sunset.

Sandra, her angelic face just inches away from my unsightly one, was beaming too. Her grin was ear to ear, but the most beautiful thing was her eyes. They were alive again! Those stunning dark brown pools sparkled and danced again; and leaked tears of joy.

We giggled like a couple of teenagers at Rendezvous and kissed again. That one lasted much longer.

As our lips separated I remembered Andy. And I think Sandra read my mind because she pulled away and we both turned to look where Andy stood by the stove.

My face-splittin' grin and Sandra's ear to ear smile didn't even compare with Andy. Below his nose that boy's head was nothin' but white, shinning teeth; his smile so big that the rest of his head had disappeared. His eyes were pushed partly shut to make room for his cheeks and even they actually glowed with happiness. His own tears of joy trickled down his face; causing muddy little paths on his cheeks as they picked up the trail dirt we hadn't had a chance to scrub off yet.

"So, I reckon its okay with you," I pulled Sandra tight, "if I get real friendly like with your momma?" I turned my gaze to the angel face beaming up at mine. "I ain't hardly thought of nothin' else for nearly three years now."

And then Andy was standing beside us, slapping me on the back with one hand and hugging his ma with the other.

"I reckon that would be just fine with me, Mount." Andy laughed. "Just fine indeed. In fact, I..."

"YOU SON OF A BITCH!"

I ain't sure which I heard first, the insane scream or the door crashing in. Suddenly Andrew Worthington the Second was standin' just inside the ruined door, weaving from side to side, and waving a six-shot revolver.

My pistol hung in its holster and unprimed on a peg beside the door under my buffalo robe.

"You can't take what's mine! I'll kill you first!"

I shoved Sandra hard to the right and Andy to the left. I didn't know where they were goin' and didn't care; as long as it was away from me.

The gun roared. I braced for the impact of the bullet, but it didn't come; instead, something far worse. I heard Sandra cry out in pain.

The barrel of the gun steadied on my chest and I didn't figure he'd miss twice from that range.

I sidestepped and dropped down on one knee as the gun went off again. I swear I felt the bullet whiz pass my ear. Another half inch lower and it would've made my right ear match the left; the one the Indian tomahawk had shortened.

I pushed off with my planted foot and went in low and fast. I grabbed Worthington's gun hand as I came up and forced it toward the ceiling. We went chest to chest and I drove him back through the doorway and out into the mud that was the alley behind the businesses.

Worthington stumbled and went down and I crashed down on top of him. I still had a grip on his gun hand, only now it was pointed along the ground and was a danger. I wrapped my big hand around his, squeezed with all my might, and slammed his hand and the gun against the ground. I heard bones breaking and a muffled scream came from underneath me. The gun tumbled from his broken hand and slid through the mud several feet away.

And then the bastard bit me! On my chest, just next to my right nipple.

It was my turn to scream as I pushed up onto my hands and knees. He was clamped on hard enough that I lifted him a foot off the ground before he lost his hold and fell back into the mud. I saw his healthy left hand reachin' for a knife that was sheathed on his belt.

From my hands and knees, I rose up and planted my right knee in his chest with all the strength and weight I had. The air rushed outta his lungs with the force of a twister. The hand that had been reachin' for the knife came up to clutch weakly at his throat, as though that'd help him breathe again. His eyes grew large with fear.

Then I hit him.

I repositioned myself so that I straddled his chest; and hit him again with every ounce of strength I could muster; the blow driven by an all consuming hatred.

I thought of the bruise on Sandra's porcelain doll face and hit him again.

I thought of Andy growin' up without a proper pa; and I hit him again.

I was suddenly jolted back to reality by the memory of Sandra's cry of pain just moments before, and it occurred to me that she could be in the cabin seriously injured, or worse.

I hit the bastard one last time, but I don't think he felt that one.

I got to my feet, took three very unsteady steps, and dropped back down onto my knees. I had to get into the cabin and check on Sandra! Even on my knees I was shaking so bad I nearly toppled over.

It only took a couple deep breaths, but it seemed like hours before I was able to climb to my feet. By that time there were several of the town's folk standing around watching me and looking down at Mr. Worthington.

I ignored them and staggered through the door and into the cabin.

"Let me go! I'm fine!" The big wingback chair had been pulled up and turned around. Sandra was sitting in it, but was determined to get out. Andy and a woman tried to hold her down. Andy also held a towel to her left arm. The towel was bloody.

When she saw me come through the door she quit fightin' and dropped back into the chair.

"Oh, thank God! Mount, are you okay?"

"Me?" My legs felt about as sturdy as dandelion stems, but I made it to one of the chairs beside the table without fallin'. "You're the one that's white as a ghost and bleedin' all over."

"The bullet just grazed my arm, I'm fine."

Andy pulled the towel away to reveal an ugly red welt across Sandra's upper arm, a couple inches above her elbow. Blood still oozed from the wound, but had mostly stopped. And damned if it wasn't the most beautiful ugly red welt I've ever seen, because it meant that Sandra wasn't seriously hurt.

Elton Raulson, proprietor, as well as bartender, of the saloon came cautiously into the cabin. It turned out that the woman helping Sandra was Elton's missus, Olivia.

Raulson looked nervously at Sandra, then at Andy, but wouldn't look at me. He made the announcement while looking at his wife.

"Mr. Worthington is dead."

A small cry escaped from Sandra and she covered her face with her hands.

Other than maybe a tightening of his expression, Andy continued to stare straight ahead.

I ain't sure what showed on my face, but I surely was a jumble of feelings inside. I felt guilty and sorry for taking a life, while at the same time I also felt relief and...yeah damn it, even a little satisfaction.

"Now, Walt Jennings over at the General Store and me are the closest thing we got to a lawman these days." Elton said. "I guess it's up to me to figure out if any wrong doing has gone on here."

He walked over so that he stood in front of Sandra.

"I'm sorry for your loss, Mrs. Worthington." He looked nervous. "Although, I have to say that I don't know how distraught you should be considering the way things have been around here lately. With Mr. Worthington and all, I mean."

Sandra's hands came away from her face. She wore a sad, even remorseful expression. Her eyes were plumb dry.

"Andrew was a good man once; even a kind and generous man, but that person died years ago." Sandra reached out and took Andy's hand in hers. "The man lying out there in the street is a stranger to us. He's not my husband or my son's father."

"Yes, ma'am." Raulson turned a nervous glance towards me, and then looked back at Sandra. "I still need to figure out what happened here. Can you, uh…can you tell me what happened here in the cabin?"

And both Sandra and Andy told Elton Raulson about how Mr. Worthington had come crashin' through the door screamin' like a drunk banshee and shooting. I told him about seeing Worthington reach for the knife on his belt.

"Well, I don't see any reason for any further legal gibberish. It appears to me a simple case of self defense." Mr. Raulson was obviously very relieved to have the investigation over.

I was suddenly so exhausted that the best I could do was to nod my head in appreciation. I was so worn out my whole body ached, and my mind couldn't focus on any one thought.

"Elton, we need to get these folks some rooms." Olivia Raulson said to her husband. She looked around the shack with obvious disgust. She gestured towards the door. "Now that…he's gone, this woman and boy can't stay here in this sorry excuse for a shelter. They'd freeze to death if we ever got a decent cold spell."

Elton looked uncomfortably at the floor. He was, after all, a businessman first. Giving room and board away for free wasn't a smart business move.

"I'm willing to work for anything we get." I said. I stood up and discovered that my legs had sturdied up some and I was hardly shakin' at all anymore. "I can do pretty much anything that needs done around here."

"Me too." Andy hurried to join in. "I'll do whatever you need Mr. Raulson. I'll do a good job too."

"Yeah," Elton looked me up and down and then over at Andy. "We can probably work something out."

And we did.

*

Sandra and Andy moved into a cozy room upstairs above the saloon. I bunked in a storage room for a couple weeks while I worked on the shack in the alley.

Mr. Raulson provided the tools and materials and I shored it up and braced it so there was no more chance of it blowin' over in a strong wind. Then I used a mixture of sawdust from the mill, and straw from a farm just outside of town, for insulation. I nailed up planks for the inside walls and new ceiling, and finished up by sealing the whole place with linseed oil inside and out.

When I got done I had myself a warm, comfortable little place to live. Just perfect for a mountain sized mountain man, with just enough space left over for any company that he might have; as long as the company wasn't more than two people.

It didn't take much persuadin' from Elton and Olivia Raulson to convince us to stay on till spring. It would've been damn near impossible with Mr. Worthington roaming around town, but with him gone we spent a right enjoyable winter in the beautiful Willamette Valley.

They buried Mr. Andrew Worthington the Second on the local Boothill. They planted him high up on the hillside, out in the sun. The lower, shaded areas were reserved for local folks, not easterners. Although, when it comes right down to it, the local folks came from back east too.

Worthington's wife and son didn't attend his funeral. As a matter of fact, if you count the gravedigger and ole Doc Portman, the town's doctor and mortician, there were exactly three people in attendance; two of 'em still among the living. Doc Portman spoke what words were necessary. They hired four local boys to help plant that pine casket in the ground.

*

Andy and I both worked hard for Elton. Even with the lack of travelers that wandered into town, there was always somethin' that needed done.

We also both helped out Walt Jennings over there at the General Store. He was now the owner of the building and the entire inventory that had once belonged to Mr. Worthington, and he needed a lot of help movin' it all into his store.

Chapter Twelve

Winter in the Willamette Valley sure ain't what this mountain man's used to back in the Rocky Mountains.

As winter rolled on it'd get a might colder, then it'd warm back up. It got wet, and then it got wetter. I swear it wasn't a question of whether it was gonna rain; it was only a matter of how hard. And when the wind picked up and commenced to gustin' down that valley along the river, it could get downright uncomfortable; although it never came close to the Rocky Mountain cold that I'd experienced; a cold so bitter that you have to thaw out your words over a fire before you know what it is you said. And all winter long we never got enough snow in the Willamette to cover a pile of horseshit.

We spent the rest of that winter workin' and preparing for spring, and our journey home. There was endless planning for the trip and endless talk and speculation about the life the three of us were going to have when we got home. I don't believe there was ever a moment's thought about not going back to my cabin in the mountains.

*

By mid-March the weather along the Willamette Valley was plenty nice enough to travel, and if the truth be known I'd plumb had my fill of both rain and town livin', and was itchin' to get back home, but I knew there would be no gettin' through the mountains that early in the spring.

One day two wagons rolled into town coming up from the south. The travelers included three men, two women, and a boy who was just a couple years younger than Andy. The two boys immediately became great friends for the rest of the time that we were there.

Sandra and the rest of the ladies in town also became good friends with the two new womenfolk. Damn near every afternoon there'd be a gaggle of women in the General Store, cackling and carryin' on.

Most importantly, one of the gentlemen was a preacher. He even had some paperwork that said so.

Doc Portman took care of all the legal necessities such as officially pronouncing Mr. Worthington dead, which made Sandra a proper widow.

And then that new preacher man presided over our wedding.

That's right!

On Sunday, March 24th, while we were spending some time alone in a little hidin' spot I'd discovered along the river, I got down on a knee and asked Sandra if she'd be my wife. She didn't hesitate for even a second before sayin' yes. Then she cried.

We were married on Thursday, March 28th 1844.

Andy and I worked hard to paint over the Worthington name on the front of that big building on Main Street. Since it was nearly empty, and given the fact that everybody in town attended, we held our wedding in the building which had once been Mr. Worthington's dream.

I tried to borrow a button-down shirt, but there wasn't one in town big enough to fit me, so I cleaned up my deerskins the best I could. Olivia Raulson trimmed up my hair and I shaved my whiskers off. I figure I looked as good as six and a half feet of ugly can look. The woman I love gazed at me like I was the most handsome man in the world. Now, I ain't sure just what she was seein', but I thank the good Lord for that look in her eyes.

My bride was radiant in a cream colored dress that belonged to one of the ladies that'd come in with the wagons. The women made some minor adjustments to the dress, and it still didn't fit perfectly, but managed to look beautiful; but then, my Sandra would look magnificent dressed in anything...or, nothing at all.

Her long black hair had gotten back its shine and life. It draped over her left shoulder and hung down in front, held together by five white ribbons and bows. There was a white flower tucked above her left ear.

Sandra had put back on a few pounds over the winter and once again had all the right curves in all the proper places. Her face had filled out and was radiantly beautiful. Her dark, mahogany eyes danced and sparkled with joy.

Andy had kept his beard, but it was trimmed up real nice as he stood up for his ma and me as witness. I think he may've been the happiest person in that room. Happier even than either Sandra or me, if that was possible.

The first time I laid eyes on Sandra on our wedding day was when she walked in through that front door, on Andy's arm, and down the aisle between all the town folk. She was, of course, dressed in her wedding finery, and all of a sudden I had trouble drawin' a breath and my knees got kinda wobbly. My ole heart began to thumpin' double-time and the blood raced through me like a flood. I was suddenly brim full of nervous energy, and I wanted to move! I felt like jumpin' up and down, or dancin' a jig, or maybe runnin' up the side of a mountain somewhere.

Instead, I stood up straight with my hands intertwined in front of me and grinned like a crazy man as I watched my stunning bride come towards me down that aisle.

Now folks, I simply can't come up with suitable words to describe how incredibly beautiful that woman was. The most magnificent Rocky Mountain sunset, or a lush, green springtime meadow filled with wildflowers, butterflies, and a majestic herd of elk, would pale next to the beauty of the lady who had agreed to be my wife.

Andy stayed in my shack. Sandra and I spent our wedding night in the upstairs room that she and Andy had been sharing. It was the most magnificent night of this ole mountain man's life.

Chapter Thirteen

It was dang near the end of April before we struck out for home, and I still wasn't sure that we could make it through the high country. If the warm weather we'd been havin' in Oregon City was any hint then I had to figure spring had arrived in the mountains too and the passes would be negotiable. I knew better than to actually count on that, but I had the itch to get goin' real bad, and just couldn't wait no longer.

Andy and I shook some hands, slapped some backs, and were happy to get on the trail.

Sandra was sadder than a water-bug on a dry rock, and had a hard time sayin' goodbye to some of those folks who'd become very good friends. There were a lot of long, lingering hugs and a bushel basket full of tears and good wishes.

Within a couple miles of town she'd shaken her melancholies and was smilin' and singin' and happy as a puppy chasin' a stick.

After leaving Oregon City it was an enjoyable day of travel back to the ferry across the Columbia. We traveled downstream with the Willamette River rushing past on our left for only a couple hours before we turned away and headed northeast. There were plenty of landmarks we remembered and we followed them right back to the LaCamas ferry.

The sun was shinin' and for a change the wind was calm. The ground, trees, and sky were all filled with slithering, scampering, and flying critters of every sort. We could see, smell, and hear spring busting out all around us.

We spooked about five head of deer out of a small stand of maple trees. At least I think they was deer. They had a reddish coat, and weren't much bigger than a full grown hound dog.

Now, packed away, very carefully packed away, were three precious bottles of whiskey. I had intended to use one of those bottles as payment to get ferried across the Columbia, but Sandra so enchanted the Barteau brothers that they ferried us across the river for nuthin' more than the promise that we'd come back again one day.

At camp that night, we each took a snort from the first bottle of whiskey just to celebrate savin' it.

Sandra's whole body shook and shuddered as her swallow burned its way from her beautiful lips down into her beautiful stomach. I kinda enjoyed watchin'. Andy and I laughed at her a little, but we did it polite like.

I quit laughin' when it was Andy's turn.

Now I know that Andy had had a taste of liquor or two in his day, after all he was already seventeen, but it kinda worried on me how he seemed to take to drinkin' like a cat to warm milk.

Andy took a couple of long pulls from that whiskey bottle and didn't hardly make a face of any sort. I've noticed over the years that some folks can develop a hankerin' for liquor that nearly takes over their lives.

I didn't offer Andy a second drink.

My intention was to cross over to the north bank of the Columbia at LaCamas because the traveling was a might easier than the southern side. And then when we got to where the river turned, where it came down from the north and bent around to head west, we'd cross back to the other side so we could drop down and skirt below the largest of the mountain ranges, but I miscalculated the weather's effects and misjudged the land.

Where we crossed, there at the LaCamas ferry, the river is fairly wide and flat. The water level was runnin' high, but the crossing was easy as wadin' a creek with the help of the ferry. I should've figured that that wouldn't be the case further upstream where the gorge was steeper and narrower.

When we got to the spot just upstream from the Wascopam Mission, where Andy and I had crossed the previous fall, the Columbia was a rushing torrent that nobody in their right mind would venture into.

We ended up having to take the harder, more mountainous route all due to the fact that I'm dumber than a danged tree stump.

The five day trip back upstream along the mighty Columbia River took us seven long days. The weather stayed warm with almost daily rainstorms.

About mid-afternoon every day you could count on the thunderclouds to start buildin' in the west, and depending on how warm it'd been that afternoon, depended on how nasty the storm was. Sometimes, on the cooler days, we just got a spit of moisture, and sometimes, when it'd been hotter, we'd end up runnin' for cover from not only the driving rain, but also dodging lightning bolts that were striking so close we could smell 'em.

Wherever there was a low spot there was runnin' water. The deeper ravines and coulees that had been dry last fall were filled with runoff. We made a couple of dangerous crossings and several long detours.

I knew two days before we got to the place where I'd planned on crossing the river that my plan wasn't going to work. Every mile we traveled the water got deeper and faster.

After seven hard days we got to that spot where the Columbia comes down from the north and bends around to the west; the spot where I'd planned to cross over to the south side. That river was lapping at the very top of its banks in a mad, whitewater dash down the gorge. There was no way we were going to cross.

So, instead of fording the river, we were forced to follow that raging current around the curve until we was travelin' due north. That put us on the west bank rather than the north, but whatever the hell you called it, it was still the wrong damn side of the river.

We traveled north for two and a half more days before we found a place where I figured we had a chance of crossin'. The land had flattened and the Columbia had spread out and slowed down considerably. I could see the mountains in the distance to the north and northwest and knew that there'd be no crossing up there.

And even with the flatter land that river was still mighty deep and dangerous. On the east side of the river we could make out some barren, dirt bluffs. They looked a mile away, although I knew that the river wasn't nearly that wide.

"Should we rope ourselves together, Mount?" Sandra asked.

We were eating some jerky and the last of the bread that we'd brought with us from Oregon City. It was a tad bit stale and we had to feed a couple of moldy pieces to the birds.

I considered Sandra's suggestion, but decided against it.

"Na, I don't think so." I studied the river lookin' for currents or rapids. It looked calm as a quiet day. "I reckon if somethin' awful would happen and one of us would drown, that'd still be better than all three of us."

And there I went again, sayin' something plumb stupid before thinkin'.

"If you would die, Mount, I..." Sandra was starin' at me real hard with a look on her face that tugged at my heart. "...I don't know if I'd *want* to live."

"Sandra, I was..."

"You damn well better not drown and leave us out here in the middle of nowhere, Mount." Andy interrupted. He had half a smile on his face and was trying to lighten the mood. "We're going to need you to hunt for us on the way home."

I laughed. Andy laughed. Sandra dipped her head, squeezed her eyes shut, and wiped a tear off her cheek.

"Ain't none of us going to die today. All we got to do is stay mounted up and let the horses do the work." I stood up and started packin' up what little we'd taken out. "Let's go get wet. Andy, you try to splash some water up there under your armpits on the way across. You could use a bath."

Despite herself, Sandra smiled.

"Okay." She stood up determinedly and headed for her horse. "Let's get this over with." And for around the thousandth time I was impressed by her grit and determination.

The weather had been mighty warm, but that water came down out of the mountains not fifty miles away, and it was still damn cold.

I had Andy and Skyhawk lead us. Sandra was in the middle, and I followed with the packhorse behind me. I'd learned my lesson, and held the packhorse's lead-rope loosely in my hand where I could drop it or it could be pulled out of my grip and not take me with it.

Skyhawk wasn't real anxious to get his feet wet, but with Andy firmly encouraging him, he plunged ahead. He got scared again a few seconds later when his feet left the ground, but he recovered quickly and swam strongly towards the opposite bank.

We were about halfway across when something spooked Sandra's mare. That horse's ears laid back, her eyes widened, and she started snortin' and pawing franticly at the water, causing her to bounce up and down and jerk from side to side. I didn't see anything in the water and am only guessing that it was a snake out for a swim.

Sandra's butt started sliding off her saddle to the right. She dropped the reins and threw her upper body over the left side of her horse's neck. She wrapped her arms around that mare and held on. In a few seconds the horse settled down and started swimming again. Sandra was able to reach the reins and settle herself back into her saddle.

I realized that I hadn't taken a breath in quite a spell and nearly fainted.

For the rest of our swim I saw terror in Sandra's eyes every time she turned to check on me; which was every couple seconds.

We were within a hundred feet of the bank when Andy suddenly burst into song and started scooping up handfuls of water and splashing them under his armpits.

I laughed until I nearly fell off Goldfire. Even Sandra was able to laugh, even if it was nervously.

We'd drifted nearly a quarter mile downstream when we finally reached the east bank.

We built us a big bonfire using dead, dry grass for tinder and driftwood to build up the fire. We stripped down to our skivvies and dried our clothes and warmed ourselves. Sandra made Andy and me turn around while she took her wet clothes off and wrapped up in a blanket.

By the time our clothes had dried we decided to spend the night. We set up camp and used the coals from our fire to cook up a welcome pot of hot soup. We had meat, potatoes, and spices with us, and I was able to find some wild greens to add.

When we was done eatin', just as the sun was settling down behind the western horizon, Sandra and I shared a couple pulls on the whiskey bottle as we watched the fire in the sky burn out. I noticed Andy eyeing the bottle, but he didn't ask, and I didn't offer him any.

It was a mighty fine evening, and we all three slept like babies wrapped in our mamma's arms.

*

That week that we traveled northeast across the plains was a joyous time. What had been dry, barren, and mostly frozen land only a month or so before was now busting out all over with spring.

We came across a shallow creek running with fresh water every few miles. Birds filled the endless blue sky and butterflies and honey bees filled the grass covered plains, enjoying the overabundance of wildflowers that'd sprung up. The smell of flower blossoms filled the already sweet spring air.

The land was mostly flat, cut with creeks and sandstone bluffs. Trees only grew here and there along the water routes.

The horses enjoyed the traveling as much as we did with a slow, easy pace and the sweet, fresh grass.

Whenever possible we rode two or three abreast. Sandra and I tried to stay close enough that we could hold hands. The three of us talked and laughed and had us a grand ole time.

Now and then Sandra and Andy would even break into song. I wasn't allowed to join in because the two of them had heard my singin' voice before.

The herds of antelope, packs of coyotes, and all the other critters that we passed out there on the plains must've thought we were plumb loco as we rode along hootin', hollerin', and singin'.

At night Sandra and I would lay our bedrolls side by side so that I could hold her and we could whisper back and forth as we drifted off to sleep watchin' the stars shine above us.

We both felt those strong urges and desires that were only natural given the circumstance, but we agreed that along the trail, with Andy layin' only a few feet away wasn't the proper time or place. Sandra had to firmly remind me that I'd agreed, several times along the way.

After a week on the plains we moved into some rolling foothills covered in pine forest and then on to the first range of the Rocky Mountains that we had to cross.

The Hudson Bay Company's Fort Colville was somewhere north of us. I'd hoped to stop there, but I didn't want to take the time to travel further than we needed to. We followed the Spokane River upstream to Lake Coeur d'Alene.

Twice I saw a small band of Indians watchin' us from higher ground; probably Spokane or Colville Indians. I never mentioned it to Sandra or Andy, and we didn't have any trouble from them.

The closer we got to the mountains the more high country snow-pack I realized was still up there; blocking the passes and creating a real danger of deadly avalanches for anyone caught below.

The weather had been unseasonably warm, and the rivers and streams were near flood levels, so I knew it wouldn't be more than a few days before enough snow would melt that we'd have a chance of making it through.

We followed the northern shore of Lake Coeur d'Alene to its eastern end. I picked a nice spot a safe distance from the rising lake, and set up camp. I planned on staying for several days.

"Hey, boy." I called to Andy. He was gathering firewood under the pine trees.

"Yeah, old man?"

"You have some respect for your elders or I'll whoop your ass, boy."

"Hell no you won't."

"You think you can take me?" I started to march across the grass towards him, fists clenched and a snarl on my face. "And watch your mouth in front of your ma." His smartass smile widened into a full fledged grin and he dropped the armload of firewood. Sandra sat beside the fire ring I'd built out of rocks and covered her mouth with both hands to hold back her laughter. When I got to within ten feet of Andy I lunged for him. He howled with delight and bolted away. I missed him by a mile.

"No, I can't fight you, but I can outrun you!"

"Not all the way back to the cabin you can't."

"Good point." He'd pulled up over beside Sandra. We all shared a laugh.

"You brought up a good point back at the Columbia." I said. Andy's laugh turned into a confused look.

"I did?"

"Yep. You remember jokin' about needing me to do the huntin'?"

"Oh, yeah."

"Any son of mine is gonna know how to provide for himself." I smiled at both of them then turned my gaze on Andy. "You and me are goin' huntin'."

His smile returned.

"Neat!"

Sandra assured me that she'd be just fine in camp alone for a couple of hours. I remembered the bands of Indians that I'd seen spyin' on us, and asked her to come along.

We didn't need to go far. I headed west a mile or so to make sure we were clear of the campfire smoke, then cut north up a pine filled draw.

I was after wapiti; some folks call 'em elk. The country was perfect for them; lots of green grass and fresh water with forest covered foothills beside miles of plains to the west.

Just as I'd hoped, when that draw leveled out it was into a fairly large clearing on the hillside. I had Sandra get comfortable down under a deadfall log and used some pine boughs to hide her. I kissed her goodbye, and told her to stay put until we came to get her.

Now, just in case any of you folks are wonderin', I ain't sayin' that a woman can't hunt. I reckon they'd be just as good at it as any man if they had a hankerin', but I ain't met many that wouldn't just as soon let their man provide the meat.

Andy and I slowly crept through the last remaining trees until we could peer out into the clearing. And sure enough, there was about twenty head of cow elk grazing in the meadow. There were maybe eight calves running and frolicking among the group. Problem was that they were a couple hundred yards away on the other side of the clearing; out of range for my flintlock long rifle.

Before we put the stalk on 'em, and while I could still whisper to Andy, I explained how to check the cow's udder to tell which ones had a calf suckling. We didn't want to shoot someone's ma.

We spent the next half hour creeping silently through the forest in a big circle around the clearing. While we were still back far enough to be hidden from the clearing I helped Andy prime the flintlock. He was shaking with excitement as he tamped the ball and powder.

Andy had done some target shootin', but not a whole lot.

Through mostly gestures I reminded Andy to breathe properly and to squeeze down on the trigger slowly, not to jerk on it. I gave him a smile and a wink, and with a nod told him to go get us a grub stake for crossin' the mountains.

He made me proud as he advanced to the edge of the clearing. He stayed behind cover and picked each footfall real careful so he didn't make a sound. There was a nice big juniper bush right at the edge of the clearing; a perfect spot to take the shot from.

Andy slowly dropped down on one knee and surveyed the band of cows that grazed less than fifty feet away. He raised the long rifle to his shoulder. I saw him pause and wondered why. Then I saw him slide forward a foot and realized that he planned to use a large branch of that juniper for a gun-rest.

Now, normally that'd be a good idea. The problem was that the branch Andy rested the heavy rifle-barrel on was dead and dry as desert sand. The weight of that gun came down on the branch and it gave way with a crack like close thunder in a lightning storm.

It took less than five seconds for those cows and calves to vanish as if they'd never existed.

Andy turned to stare at me with shock and horror in his wide eyes. I swallowed a laugh as I went to join him. I pointed out the difference in color of the needles on the dead juniper branch as compared to the live branch. I assured him that it was a mistake that could've happened to anyone.

We turned to head back to where Sandra waited. I froze and grabbed Andy's shoulder. I pointed, and he looked to see a lone cow standing only a hundred feet away in amongst the trees. She must've wandered away from the rest of the herd. When they ran, she knew something was going on, but she didn't know what. She was confused and just stood there looking around.

There was a fallen cottonwood to our left. I pointed it out to Andy and then slowly lowered myself to a knee.

Andy sidestepped behind me until he was hidden by the cottonwood. He crept, bent over, along behind the trunk of the huge tree to its end. He slowly rose up and rested the rifle across the tree trunk.

From where he was, it was about a seventy-five foot shot, and Andy couldn't have made it any better. The ball entered just behind her ribs and embedded in her vitals. She was dead before she realized that she'd been shot.

Andy was grinnin' like a rodeo clown as we headed over to where the dead elk lay. The closer we got, the smaller his smile became. When we stood beside the carcass lookin' down on her glazed over eyes, tongue hangin' in the dirt, and blood oozing from the hole in her side, Andy wasn't grinnin' at all.

"Wow." He turned towards me. His eyes were brimming. "Is it weird to feel sad, Mount?"

"Nope." I laid my arm across his shoulders. "I've killed hundreds of critters over the years, and have felt bad for every single one of 'em. For a respectful man, takin' the life of anything is a hard thing to do, but it's just the way of things out here. If you want to live, well, sometimes you have to kill. Whether that be to protect yourself or your loved ones from another person, or to provide food." I slapped him on the shoulder. "Let's go get your ma, and then we'll get to work. Believe me, in a few minutes that dead elk will just be a slab of meat."

I helped Andy slit the wapiti's throat open and we left her to bleed out while we went to fetch Sandra.

Now I ain't gonna bore, or sicken, you folks with a detailed description of my teachin' Andy how to gut out and butcher that critter, but it was the most I'd laughed in a long time; and that's sayin' something, 'cause like I've explained, we'd been doin' us a whole lot of laughing on the trail.

When he reached his bloody hands up into that carcass and grabbed a hold of that jugular vein and started tuggin', trying to pull it outta the…well, never mind. I laughed till my stomach hurt, and then went and showed him a little trick my pa had taught me.

Sandra and Andy weren't real sure if they could eat any elk meat after what they'd seen, but as those back-strap steaks was cookin' over those hot coals and the juices started seepin', my wife and son's attitudes changed as their nostrils twitched and their mouths began to water. The two of them dug in like they hadn't eaten in a month.

We stayed put for four or five days. Andy and I skinned the cow and started scraping the hide. After I showed them how, Sandra and Andy took charge of stripping and smoking the meat. I built us a two-chamber smoker out of green poles and pine boughs. We found some apple wood and used wood chips from that.

By the time the meat was all smoked and dried and we were ready to move on there had been a noticeable change in the mountains. The temperature had stayed especially warm and all the runoffs that emptied into Coeur d'Alene Lake were down considerably from when we'd set up camp. I could even look up into those high mountain passes and see with my naked eye that there was considerably less snow pack.

We packed up what had been a mighty fine camp, and the next day, just as the sun's first light was a faint glow above the eastern ridge, on a warm spring morning, we headed into the mountains and towards home.

Except for a couple anxious moments when Sandra's fear of heights reared its ugly head, the five days it took for our mountain crossing went as well as I could've hoped.

Considering all the problems Andy and I'd had during our trip out to Oregon City, I would've bet the moon there'd be troubles on our return trip, but there really wasn't.

Wood for the campfire was a little short a couple nights up in the high-country, above tree line. We was forced to snuggle up real tight and hug and cuddle for warmth. I didn't mind.

I let Sandra wear my buffalo robe (which she disappeared into) for warmth. Let me tell you folks, tryin' to cozy up to a small woman wearin' a huge buffalo robe and a rabbit-fur hat pulled down tight, ain't an easy task.

Goldfire had to bust a trail thru three-foot deep snowdrifts over the highest pass, and due to all the runoff the rock got slipperier than goat snot in a few places, but all the horses did just fine and dandy, and we made the trip without a hitch.

The packhorse I led had the worst of it. She was loaded down with not only the jerked elk meat, but plenty of other provisions; coffee, sugar, salt, flour, beans, and a hundred more pounds of supplies.

One of the biggest difficulties we faced on that mountain leg of our journey was merely to remember to keep movin'. Several times we found ourselves stopped and simply staring around at the indescribable beauty of the land; each of us pointing out a more incredible, a more stunning vista than the last one.

Towering ponderosa pines framed the majestic, snow-covered peaks and bright blue sky. Waterfalls cascaded down the rock faces and creeks rushed through the pine forest in a hundred different places.

We spooked whole herds of deer and elk on a regular basis. Twice we stopped and watched, from a safe distance, as a sow black bear and her cubs played and fed in meadows.

So, fresh game and clean water were plentiful all along the route, and the weather cooperated as much as springtime weather can be expected to in the Rockies.

We were forced to take cover and hide from a couple of mean thunderstorms, and even had to seek shelter under a low overhang to wait out a short, but powerful, late-season snowstorm, but for the most part that whole danged trip home from Oregon City was a joyful adventure.

Traveling through that breathtakingly spectacular country with the incredibly beautiful woman that I loved (I still couldn't believe she was my wife), and the boy that I already thought of as my own, I was about as happy as a feller can get.

I figure it must've been around the middle of May when we crossed the continental divide. Two days later we dropped down into the upper end of the Yellowstone River Valley. We were within two days of home.

But I had me a plan.

As bad as I was itchin' to get back to my cabin with my new family, I decided on a little side trip first. You folks remember those hot springs that I'd stopped at to soak my achin' bones before gettin' home to find Andy? Well, I decided to share that particular spot with my new kin.

Like I said, I had a plan.

So, we actually followed the Yellowstone River downstream past the spot where we'd turn to go home. We got to the hot springs about mid-afternoon. I set up camp back behind some trees that grew on the grassy knoll above the sandstone cliffs where the hot water poured from to fill the pools below. From camp the hot pots were below the slope of the hill and out of sight.

After setting up the campsite, the three of us strolled down to the hot springs to soak. We all wore britches and shirts into the water, which was only proper. Sandra and Andy were delighted with the place and both agreed that, anxious as we were to get to the cabin, it was well worth the short delay.

That evening, after enjoying some delicious rabbit stew mixed with fresh greens, all three of us took another short soak before we went up to camp, stoked up the fire to a healthy blaze, and settled down into our bedrolls.

Just as I'd counted on, Andy was snoring lightly before I even needed to add wood to the fire.

In the glow of the flames I saw Sandra's eyes sparkling at me from just a few feet away. Her face was lit with a golden glow, and the fire danced through her raven hair. She was grinning from ear to ear.

I slipped out of my blanket, took Sandra by the hand, and quietly led her away from the camp and down to those pools filled with hot water.

We didn't bother with clothes that time around.

Now folks, I'm too much of a gentleman to go into detail about what went on in and around those hot springs that night, but I *can* say that it was a whole heap better than I'd even imagined; and what I'd imagined had been pretty damned spectacular.

Sandra and I spent the entire night down at the hot springs. When we was too exhausted to do anything else, we just spent time lounging in each others arms. We may've even dozed off a time or two, but we didn't get much sleep. The next day on the trail we were tired to the bone, and about as happy as two people can get.

It was late in the forenoon when we turned north, away from the Yellowstone River, and followed Sweetgrass Creek up into my valley. I figured I'd burst with excitement.

When we rode around that left hand bend in the creek, there by the three big cottonwoods, and my cabin came into view, I did explode.

"Yaaaa whooouuu!" And suddenly Goldfire and I were galloping full-out up the creek. "Yip, yip, yaaa whooo!"

We skidded to a stop in front of the cabin, I turned to see if Sandra and Andy had kept up.

My heart froze when I saw that they'd stopped. At about the spot where Goldfire and I had broken into a run, Sandra and Andy stood still.

"Now that we're here, is Sandra figurin' she made a mistake?" I was suddenly sure that for whatever reason, Sandra didn't want to come any closer to my cabin. *"Or have they both decided this wasn't right? Are they having doubts?"*

I was nervous as a skitter-bug, but I nudged Goldfire and we hurried back to where my wife and son sat motionless; well nearly. As I got closer I saw that Sandra was crying.

"What?" I pulled up beside her so I could lay a worried hand on her shoulder. "What is it, my dear? What's wrong?" I held my breath as I waited for her answer.

She took a deep shuddering breath and blew it out. She turned to me and smiled through her tears.

"Oh, Mount," She looked back up the valley towards our cabin and the meadow, foothills, and majestic mountain peaks that stretched out behind it. "It's so beautiful! It's the most beautiful place I've ever seen!"

Andy too had tears leakin' from his eyes; and was grinning wider than the sky.

"Well now, Ma'am," I was so relieved that my knees shook a bit as I stood up in my stirrups and leaned over far enough so I could kiss a tear off of Sandra's cheek. "I'm mighty happy to hear you say that, seein' how this here is gonna be your home for the next fifty years or so."

"Well then," Sandra wiped the tears from her eyes and sat up straight in the saddle. "Let's go home, shall we?"

And off she went, urging that big bay mare up to a full gallop. Andy and Skyhawk were right behind her. They both rode like they'd been born in a saddle. I nearly burst with pride.

Goldfire and I could've easily overtaken them, but we didn't.

I let my wife and son beat me home.

CPSIA information can be obtained
at www.ICGtesting.com
Printed in the USA
LVHW05s2331100918
589767LV00002B/301/P